THE DESERT WILL REJOICE
and blossom as the rose

**THE STORY OF THE FULFILMENT OF
A THREE-PART PROPHECY GIVEN IN 1987
ABOUT THE CITY OF BIRMINGHAM**

Christine Parkinson

Moorlands College Library (MM)

MM00250

Authors On Line

Visit us online at www.authorsonline.co.uk
IMC Library

An AuthorsOnLine Book

Copyright © Authors OnLine Ltd 2004

Text Copyright © Christine Parkinson 2004

Cover design by Siobhan Smith ©

All rights reserved. No part of this publication may be reproduced, stored in a retrieval system, or transmitted in any form or by any means, electronic, mechanical, photocopy, recording or otherwise, without prior written permission of the copyright owner. Nor can it be circulated in any form of binding or cover other than that in which it is published and without similar condition including this condition being imposed on a subsequent purchaser.

ISBN 0 7552 0113 2

Authors OnLine Ltd
40 Castle Street
Hertford SG14 1HR
England

This book is also available in e-book format, details of which are available at www.authorsonline.co.uk

ABOUT THE AUTHOR

Dr Christine Parkinson studied as a biologist and spent the first part of her career in medical research. In 1984, she moved to Birmingham's inner city, to follow a call that God had placed on her life, to minister to the poor and socially excluded of the inner city and to fight for social justice.

In Birmingham, she worked as Urban Missioner to 12 inner city Baptist churches for six years and then, in 1993, began as community organiser to the Jericho Community Project, in Balsall Heath, an inner city suburb of Birmingham. This role enabled her to have direct involvement in the development of two of the projects described in this book. Dr Parkinson is also committed to following a contemplative prayer life. This is her second full-length book. The first, also published by Authors On Line, is entitled "I will lift up my eyes".

Author's Notes

This book contains several quotations from the Bible. In each case, the version from which the quotation has been taken is included as an abbreviation, in brackets after the reference, as follows:

(LB) The Living Bible © Tyndale House Publishers, 1971
(NIV) New International Version © International Bible Society, 1980
(NLT) New Living Translation © Tyndale Charitable Trust, 1996

TABLE OF CONTENTS

CHAPTER AND TITLE	PAGE
Prologue	1
Chapter 1: Gilgal!	5
Chapter 2: Reversals!	44
Chapter 3: Jericho!	49
Chapter 4: Bethel!	94
Chapter 5: Drawing the three parts together	105

"THE DESERT WILL REJOICE"

PROLOGUE

Many significant Christian leaders have visited the city of Birmingham in the West Midlands during the last two decades. They have come from all over the world and several have perceived that God is about to send a new outpouring of his Holy Spirit into the city. They believe that this will turn the city around, so that it becomes a beacon of light throughout the UK and the world, causing many people to commit their lives to Jesus.

The reality for the city in this year of 2004 is very different. Vast areas of the city have become strongholds of Islam and much of the city is given over to drug dealing, violence, prostitution, crime and corruption. There are gang cultures, street crime, regular shootings and murder. Hundreds of asylum seekers (some legal and others not) have sought refuge and anonymity in the city. Many families are in poverty, living in poor quality housing; thousands are addicted to drugs, some living rough on the streets, finding their food from bins; thousands more are unemployed, and have been for years, and there is violence within families too, affecting the lives of many women and their children. And in the city there is a prison, vastly overcrowded, accommodating many others who have been caught up in these destructive cultures - a prison over which hangs a heavy spirit of grief which, in many ways, could be described as symptomatic of the whole city.

So, is there hope? Are we to believe the prophetic words of the international Christian visitors about the city of Birmingham? Is the Lord going to come and suddenly turn around the lives of people living here, so that thousands bow the knee at the name of Jesus? It is quite clear that, during the 1970's to 1990's, God has been sending new people to Birmingham, to support and encourage the work of the beleaguered churches of the city, in a similar way to how he sent Christians from the West Indies to the inner city two to three decades earlier (then, to prevent many of the churches from closing). In 1984, I was one of the people that the Lord sent to Birmingham. Others sent about that time included Kees and Maria Blom, who came from Holland, Ken and Maggie Hazel, who came from Devon, David and Janet Harmer, who came from Kent, Salim and Shamim Stephen, who came from Ludhiana in India, Jane Gallagher, who came from Dorset and Eileen MacDonald and Pearl Barnes, who had earlier come from Jamaica. God has used all of these people in the setting up of the Gilgal and Jericho Projects in the city, as well as others (Revs. Bill Dixon and John Mallard and other people from various churches) who were already living here.

This book describes a three-fold prophecy, given to Maria Blom in 1987. And it shows how this prophecy began to be worked out in miraculous ways, becoming far larger than any human mind could have imagined. The projects arising from the prophecy (Gilgal, Jericho and Bethel) have turned around the lives of many hurting people in the city, but there is still so much to be done to turn the city around, so that a spirit of grief becomes a spirit of joy.

I found myself becoming a part of this three-fold prophecy, and one instrument of its outworking, and so I have told the story from my own perspective. As each part of the prophecy came about, God envisioned and motivated his people, demonstrating the miraculous through each project, strengthening the faith of his people and using the projects as a witness to his ongoing presence in the city.

The story started for me in 1983, when I was 40 years old, the Lord called me to leave my home in West London and to go to live in Birmingham. I had just been offered a job there, which I wouldn't have touched with a barge pole, left to my own devices, but I felt I should seek guidance from the Lord about whether I should take the job and move to Birmingham.

That's when he spoke to me through Isaiah 35, with the words:

"The desert will rejoice and blossom as the rose."

The moment I read those words, I knew in my spirit that God wanted me to take that step into the unknown. It was as if the words somehow became a part of me – and they have done so ever since, for I have never forgotten them – even though I didn't really understand at that point what God was meaning through them. But, I believed the words to be confirmation to me that God wanted me to move to Birmingham, even though I knew nothing about the city, was not enamoured with the secular job I had been offered and had no family roots in the city.

Not long before that, God had called me to obedience in him (see "I Will Lift Up My Eyes": Christine Parkinson; Authors on Line, Hertford, UK, 2002) so, despite my uncertainty about the job, I left London and moved to Birmingham in early 1984.

Now, 20 years later, I can look back and see how he has fulfilled his promise in Isaiah 35 and this is why I have written this book and entitled it after that text. The book is divided into chronological sections, which show the outworking of God's purposes in the city through miraculous revelations, confirmations, divine appointments and abundant provision of resources. Each story is very different but will speak for itself.

"The desert and the parched land will be glad;
the wilderness will rejoice and blossom.
Like the crocus, it will burst into bloom;
It will rejoice greatly and shout for joy.
The glory of Lebanon will be given to it,
the splendour of Carmel and Sharon;
they will see the glory of the Lord, the splendour of our God.

Strengthen the feeble hands, steady the knees that give way;
Say to those with fearful hearts,
'Be strong, do not fear; your God will come,
he will come with vengeance; with divine retribution
he will come to save you.'

Then will the eyes of the blind be opened
and the ears of the deaf unstopped.
Then will the lame leap like a deer, and the mute tongue shout for joy.
Water will gush forth in the wilderness and streams in the desert.
The burning sand will become a pool, the thirsty ground bubbling springs.
In the haunts where jackals once lay, grass and papyrus will grow.

And a highway will be there: it will be called the Way of Holiness.
The unclean will not journey on it;
It will be for those who walk in that Way;
Wicked fools will not go about on it.
No lion will be there, nor will any ferocious beast get up on it;
They will not be found there.
But only the redeemed of the Lord will walk there,
And the ransomed of the Lord will return.
They will enter Zion with singing; everlasting joy will crown their heads.
Gladness and joy will overtake them, and sorrow and sighing will flee away."

Isaiah 35 (NIV)

CHAPTER ONE

Gilgal!

*"Your people will rebuild the ancient ruins and
will raise up the age-old foundations;
you will be called Repairer of Broken Walls,
Restorer of Streets with Dwellings."*
Isaiah 58:12 (NIV)

It was a cold morning in 1987, and somewhat overcast, as I drove along the busy road to a meeting at my church. But, even though the weather was dreary, I was in good spirits. It was one of those rare days when I felt so close to the Lord, that my whole being (thoughts, words and actions) seemed to flow in harmony with his Spirit, in tune with his voice and his leading, rather than being directed by my own whims. My eyes must have been on the road (out of habit) but my mind was with the Lord.

Suddenly, I distinctly heard a voice speaking to me:

"That's the Place!"

I looked across to see what I was passing and saw a large, very derelict, building that, many years earlier, had once been three shops with accommodation above. The shop signs were still there – a launderette, a coffee and snack bar and a piano shop – but the whole building was now falling down, dirty and exposed to the elements. Part of it had even been destroyed by fire and the charred roof timbers were pointing skywards, now devoid of tiles. It was a sad, miserable wreck of a building.

"That's the Place!"

It came as an exclamation; God's voice – an imperative, unmistakably drawing my attention to the building. There was no question in my mind that God was telling me that he wanted us to use this building in some way for his purposes. I have never been more positive about anything in my whole life!

"....his word in my heart is like a fire that burns in my bones, and I can't hold it in any longer."
Jeremiah 20: 9 (LB)

So certain was I that this was a command from God that I shared the experience with my pastor, Rev. Bill Dixon, and later with the deacons and the church meeting of my own church, for this derelict building was situated very close to the church. In the meantime I had sought from the Lord how he wanted the buildings used and I had some leading from him that it would be a place for women in need and their children.

THE DERELECT BUILDING FROM THE BACK

Unfortunately, my enthusiasm to use this derelict wreck of a building for God's purposes was not shared at first by the rest of the church, most of whom could not understand my certainty about God's voice speaking to me. All they could see was the amount of effort and money it would take to repair it and then to use it. One particular sceptic at the church meeting told me in no uncertain terms:

"You realise that we'd have to pay Poll Tax (now Council Tax) on it!"

He hadn't heard a word of the vision I had shared, nor caught my enthusiasm, nor seen God behind it. He thought it was something I had dreamed up myself – and in his eyes, it was therefore totally impractical.

But the deacons were open to spend time apart in prayer together, seeking God's guidance on the matter and I joined them for this prayer day in some trepidation. The group started by praising God in song and worship, then they entered a spirit of prayerfulness and waited on him in quietness. Almost immediately, I felt God's gentle presence touching me again, reassuring and comforting. Then, a picture flooded into my mind, as vivid as it would be in real life. I could see the derelict, piano-shop building, its roof open and exposed to the elements. And, as I watched, the burnt and broken roof timbers were replaced, with roof tiles on top of them in neat rows, as the building was renewed to a sparkling state of restoration. I was so shocked and overwhelmed by this picture, that tears started to flow.

"Lord," I whispered, "I did not want you to show me this picture. Could you show it to somebody else, so that they can believe it as strongly as I do." I started sobbing uncontrollably but the picture remained, as clear as if it had been on a screen before me. Then Ken, one of the deacons, said:

"I feel that we need to put out a fleece, as Gideon did in the Bible. Something that will confirm to us with no uncertainty that this is of the Lord."

Almost before he had finished speaking, Eileen, one of the deacons who had come from Jamaica years before, began to share quietly:

"I can see a whole crowd of people. People with all kinds of needs. They are thronging together on the pavement outside the piano-shop building. And the Lord Jesus is there among them. He is going from one to another, touching them and they are being healed. They are all coming to him to be touched and healed."

Wow! Eileen's words were a confirmation, not in the way that I had asked the Lord to provide, but in a much more powerful way. He is such a gracious God!

We didn't know it then but these pictures were only the beginning of a series of revelations and miracles that God was to bring to the church.

The events of this prayer day remain a significant memory for many of the people there but, for the next two years, not much happened. We tried to get things moving by finding out who owned the place and seeing if he was prepared to sell. The elderly Jewish owner lived in Jersey but he was not accepting offers for his run-down property – he sent a short, curt letter saying this. There was therefore no progress at all in taking the project forward - a brick wall was preventing any progress. Nothing. A complete blockage. And I am ashamed to admit that I gave up on the whole thing. The initial scepticism had been bruising – and now this brick wall. There was no money for the restoration of the building anyway and no response from the owner. It seemed such a huge task and people returned to their other agendas. The piano-shop vision had almost, but not quite, died a death.

What I did not realise then was that the Lord often uses reversals to ensure that everybody involved in a situation realises that God is behind it and is making it happen and that it doesn't come about through our own strength and vision. He does this to keep us humble, to build up our faith and to teach us to trust him (see Chapter 2).

Then, one morning in December 1989, during an early morning prayer session at Ken and Maggie's house, Bill Dixon said to me,

"I've been speaking to a colleague, Andrew, who has expertise in developing Christian building and social projects. I told him about the piano shop and he's very interested in coming to look at it, later today, and to advise us about it. Would you be free to come and meet him?"

I agreed with some reluctance and Andrew duly arrived, a man of great enthusiasm. But, rather than bombarding us with all the negative comments we had heard before, he went to see the building, stepped right inside it, clambering over fallen timbers, joists, piles of jagged bricks and accumulated rubbish, showing no fear. Then, he uttered the following, unforgettable, words:

"They used to make their buildings strong and sound in Victorian times, didn't they? I think this place could be restored safely."

I had been afraid to step inside the building, for fear that the whole lot would come down on top of me but he was remarking on how strong it looked! Later, out on the broad pavement, Andrew began to reflect:

"You know, I'm sure I've heard my colleague, Peter, talking about a derelict place like this. Another group of Christians have been asking him to develop it for them. I've got a feeling it's the same building. Have you met this group?"

We knew nothing about them and so Andrew gave us Peter's phone number. Peter confirmed that the group of Christians he was in touch with was interested in the same derelict building and so a meeting was arranged with them. They were from a small fellowship, run by a Dutch couple, which met in a nearby community centre. I went with Eileen to meet the pastor, Kees Blom, and his wife, Maria, in their home.

Eileen often tells me how she will never forget that meeting. Maria was lying on the sofa, laid low with a chronic back problem and Kees was studying in another room. At first, Maria was reluctant to talk to us, or to tell us anything about their plans (she later told us that this was because she thought somebody else had told us about it and that we wanted to steal the idea!). Whilst sensing a spirit of resistance, Eileen and I ploughed ahead, so excited were we that another Christian group was interested in the same building. We explained to Maria exactly how the Lord had spoken to us and about the pictures that we had received since. When she heard the story, Maria's attitude immediately changed and she began to praise the Lord. We ended the evening praying together, being completely filled with the Holy Spirit and praising God together. We then agreed that the two fellowships should meet together regularly, to pray the vision into reality and it was not until we started praying together that all the blockages were removed and the project started to move forward.

About that time, Maria wrote down her vision in a little booklet, so that it could be shared with others. She, too, had encountered similar blockages to me. Her story went as follows:

"We came to England, from Holland, in 1983, to study at the Birmingham Bible Institute. We felt that God had called us to study His Word and also to learn the English language. After Birmingham Bible Institute, we asked the Lord to show us what work he wanted us to do. He directed us to S [note – a suburb of Birmingham]......,where Kees has been the Pastor of the S....... Christian Fellowship...... since March 1986.

3rd April 1986

After praying for S......., I received a revelation from the Lord. He showed me a picture of a large house with three roofs. The highest roof was on the left and there was a slightly lower roof on the right, with a small roof in between. There was also land at the back belonging to the house, so that the house also had a back entrance.

I drew the house as the Lord showed me. My husband, Kees, then went searching for the house and found it, just as I had drawn it......... We were amazed. We claimed the houses and the land, that in time to come it would all be used by the Lord.

We went to several places to try and find the owner's address. Nobody could help us. Eventually, we went to the Rates Office. They couldn't help us because for the last two years everything had been put on computer and there was no record of this house......The City Treasury was unable to provide any more information. Next we visited the estate *agents who had last been dealing with this property.....We waited half a day but in the end, they withheld all the information. We next informed Dr Martin Robinson, Secretary to the Churches of Christ, of the vision and to pray about it. He gave us the name of Peter Combellack, who could perhaps help us to find the name of the owner through his many contacts. As a result of this, on 9th May 1986, we received the owner's name.... On 30th May, Peter promised to help us acquire this property.*

We prayed and asked the Lord to give us a scripture as confirmation of whether we should proceed with the whole business. The Lord made it clear through His Word that we were not to wait for people to achieve our aim, but expect the Lord to bring about His purpose.

4th December 1987

It became clear to me, after a sermon I heard, that the property was to be called GILGAL (from Joshua 4-5) and from this place would come two others:

JERICHO – Needs God's blessing (to help people with problems).

BETHEL – The house of the presence of God (people who want to know more about the Lord and to receive Him).

Gilgal was a new beginning for the people of Israel.

Peter mentioned in our first meeting that he had a charity called "New Beginnings". It seemed to be more than coincidence that both Peter and I had used the same name "New Beginnings" in our first meeting together. We felt that the Lord was speaking to us through this.

20th January 1988

Peter arranged a meeting with ...... (owner of premises) who promised to send a floor plan of the house. We have never received it.

After this, there was a long silence.

Then suddenly, out of the blue, we received a telephone call from Dr Christine Parkinson. She wanted to visit us in connection with the properties...

Our first meeting was on 30th January 1990. She came, with another sister, to our house. The Lord had also spoken to Christine, when she passed the property one day, saying clearly that He wanted to use this for His purpose...

19th June 1990

There was a beautiful unity in prayer. Since May 1990, we have been meeting together as two fellowships for prayer. We will continue to pray until the Lord answers.

The Lord has shown us very clearly how the properties are to be used. Gilgal is to be an open place, where everyone is welcome. It should have a 'homely' atmosphere, so that people feel comfortable...

The rooms upstairs will provide accommodation for women with or without children who, for one reason or another, perhaps because of their Christian faith, have lost their home or are in some form of distress and in need of help. These women would be taught skills to enable them to become self-supporting and gain in self-confidence.

The staff working on this project will receive a salary so that they have no financial worries."

It is interesting to see from Maria's story that God gave her the three part prophecy (with the three names for three new projects) in 1987, about the same time as he spoke to me as I was passing the building, and that there was also a period from 1988 to 1990 when there was no progress for them – nothing happened. And there had been a similar experience for us during the same period. It was not until the two fellowships made contact with each other, and started praying together, that things began to move. This must have been God's timing.

The joint prayer meetings between the two fellowships were very significant and blessed times, during which we experienced the pouring out of the Holy Spirit in abundance. Then one day, whilst on her way to a prayer meeting about the project, Eileen had a vision. She was walking along under some trees, which were dropping their leaves, which were crunching under her feet. As she watched the leaves, she saw that they were a golden colour, in fact not leaves at all but golden bank notes. She shared the picture with the prayer group, who were much encouraged by it for, if this project was to get off the ground, there would be a need for a great deal of golden bank notes!

But the Lord also wanted to see willingness in the body of his people to take ownership of the project. We were by now very much aware of the story of Gilgal in Joshua chapter 4, in which, when the waters of the River Jordan parted (as God had promised they would), twelve stones were taken from the bed of the river and placed to make a monument on the other side, to signify the miracle of the Lord, in opening up the waters. The monument at Gilgal was to remind future generations of God's miracle in bringing the people of Israel across the River Jordan.

> *"Then Joshua explained the purpose of the stones: 'In the future,' he said, 'when your children ask why these stones are here and what they mean, you are to tell them that these stones are a reminder of this amazing miracle – that the nation of Israel crossed the river Jordan on dry ground!'"*
> Joshua 4: 21-22 (LB)

When we studied this Bible story in church, one church member (John Wiltshire, a pensioner) shared that he thought the Lord was saying that things would go forward once the first stone had been carried (by us) across the Jordan (in figurative terms). The church deacons therefore decided that it was time for real decisions to be made, regarding funding, setting up a steering group to develop the project, finding a person to work with us in developing it and in making a firm offer to the owner. Andrew's colleague, Peter Combellack, was to help us in the initial development of the premises. Another church member gave a donation to pay for the valuation of the premises.

The owner was contacted again, and the vision shared with him, but he still showed no interest in selling. A visit was then made to the city council Urban Renewal department, to see whether we might qualify for a grant, if we were successful in obtaining the property. Unfortunately, this department was due to be disbanded but the officer there was very interested in our plans. He offered to write to the owner, telling him that, unless the property was repaired in the very near future, the City Council would take legal action to enforce repair work under the Public Health Act. Not long after this letter was sent, to my great surprise, in November 1990, I received a telephone call at home from the owner. He stated simply that he was prepared to sell the premises to us and asked us to make him an offer. I was bowled over by this call (all the way from Jersey), as my belief that the Lord was at work was still very weak. Was this to be the second great surprise about things going on in the background, of which we were totally unaware?

The premises had been valued at £40,000 and so an offer was made for this amount. We were unaware then that other people, who were not Christians, were also interested in buying and that the owner was touting for the best offer.

Then, whilst waiting for a response to the offer, a 'For Sale' board appeared outside the premises. Confused, an enquiry was made with the estate agent, and it was found that a local man, Mr R., had placed it on the market and was asking for offers. He had already received three offers for the property, one of them for £90,000! It was assumed that he had bought the premises under our noses from the original owner and now wanted to resell; we thought we had been gazumped! It seemed like we had lost the building and that this was the end of the project. All hope seemed to have gone. But God challenged us to have faith in him. Did we have enough faith to believe that he was behind this project, to be prepared to pay an inflated price for a semi-derelict property and out-bid the other offers? And, though we had no money as yet, it was agreed that Maria and I would go to the estate agents and put in an offer of £91,000 for the property. And we kept praying.

When Peter heard about the 'For Sale' board, he smelt a rat and he phoned the original owner in Jersey, with whom he had been negotiating, and found out that, in reality, the property had not been sold to Mr R. at all. Mr R. was trying to pull a fast one, by selling the buildings before he actually owned them. When the real owner in Jersey heard what Mr R. had done, he was so angry he agreed to sell to us quickly, even though we could not offer as high a sum as Mr R. had.

During this time of confusion (which I believe to be another time of reversal), the Lord prepared us to think sacrificially about the project and to make an offer to the owner for £80,000, which he accepted. And God was also at work during this time to make, not only the purchase price available to us, but also the cost of complete refurbishment of the premises. It happened in an amazing way.

Firstly, during a church meeting there was a unanimous decision to commit all of the church's reserve trustee funds to pay the deposit on the premises and the cost of developing a project there.

Then one day, I was praying about our need for the £80,000 to buy the premises, when I felt that the Lord was saying,

"If 80 people gave £1,000 each, then you would have the money you need."

This was confirmed during the Tuesday church meeting, when John Wiltshire stood up and said he thought the Lord had been saying to him exactly the same thing. John challenged 80 people in the congregation to be prepared to give £1,000 each, or 40 to give £2,000, or 160 to give £500 each. I believe that it was a challenge that the Lord had laid on both of our hearts. The deacons discussed this and then Ken, on their behalf, asked people to pledge what they could afford as loans or gifts, to the church, to enable us to secure the premises.

I was brought to tears again by what happened next. I was so touched by the faith that was shown by so many of the church members. Several old-age pensioners wrote out cheques to the church from their life savings, as well as many other generous gifts. I felt responsible for this, being one of the original visionaries, but I also felt blessed that the earlier scepticism had been replaced by sacrificial generosity and such strong faith. These responses all happened within the space of about five days.

Ken organised all of this and met the following Monday with another deacon and trustee, Derek, to count up all the money received through the pledges and cheques, as well as £30,000 from the church trustees, which represented the whole of the church reserves. The money available came to exactly the right amount! Then, just as they had finished counting, the telephone rang. It was Bill, the pastor, who was calling to say that a housing association, of which he was a board member, had just agreed to buy the premises outright and to pay for their refurbishment. Therefore, all the cheques could be torn up and returned!

What a dramatic turnaround! It was another one of God's precious coincidences. It had all happened this way. Bill had arrived at a committee meeting for the housing association a little early. The chief executive was also there early and he said to Bill,

"You don't know of a "special needs" housing project that could get off the ground quickly do you, because I've got £376,000 to spend before the end of the financial year, or lose it. Another project that was due to be funded has collapsed."

Bill could not believe his ears and explained that, yes, there was a project that he knew about and explained about the vision for the derelict premises. The chief executive agreed to go ahead with this and it was after the meeting that Bill had phoned Ken and Derek with his wonderful news. Bill himself was so bowled over by it that he announced it in church the following Sunday morning and suggested that the whole congregation get down on their knees to thank God for his provision – and this is what they did! It was an astonishing moment.

God had used another reversal to challenge us and to increase our faith. He had turned around scepticism and replaced it with sacrificial giving. What a wonderful God he is! He was also confirming for us that he was behind it all – he was in charge of the finances and the timing of the project.

> *"As the rain and snow come down from heaven, and do not return to it without watering the earth and making it bud and flourish, so that it yields seed for the sower and bread for the eater, so is my word which goes out from my mouth: it will not return to me empty, but will accomplish what I desire and achieve the purpose for which I sent it."*
> Isaiah 55: 10-11 (NIV)

A deposit was made for the property (all in faith, as the housing association took time to finalise their negotiations with us and would not go ahead until planning permission had come through), contracts were exchanged and a date for completion set for July 1991. Not long after this, negotiations began with the housing association for a partnership arrangement. They would buy and refurbish the property and we would run a housing project there upstairs, as their agents. The three shop units would be repaired and rented out to us for complementary use. They were to be let to us at a low rental for five years, after which we would have to find the full commercial rental.

About this time, John W. also shared with the fellowship another picture he had received whilst at prayer; he believed that this picture had been sent to challenge the church about their commitment to the community. In his picture, he saw the entire congregation seated in a room like an airport lounge; it was a place with big windows and views outside. Outside, there were crowds of people of every nationality but they were poor people, who had nothing, whilst the people inside had plenty. None of the people inside seemed to notice those outside, apart from one woman, who found a small door and went outside to help the people there. Through this picture, God was clearly challenging the church to build on its commitment to the local community.

This all happened during 1991, two years after the meeting with Andrew at the derelict premises and four years after the Lord had first spoken to me and to Maria independently. But, there was still to be another three years of development before the premises could be used. A steering group (comprised of people from both fellowships) met together regularly to plan for their use and another Peter, Peter White, took over negotiations with the housing association. Architectural plans for the refurbishments were drawn up, to decide on how the premises would be used. Other similar Christian projects in London were visited, to see how they organised and ran their work. A small Oasis team, placed at the church at that time to help in their mission, did some research on the pavement outside the premises, asking local people how would they like the premises to be used. Maggie used her artistic skills to design a logo for the project, which was based on the building of the Gilgal monument using stones from the bed of the River Jordan.

Another person, Shirley, a member of a Jubilee team who was placed with the church for a while, also helped, by carrying out a survey of the needs of the area, with a view to making decisions about how to use the three shop units. There were so many possibilities: to reopen the launderette and make it a place where people could have a chat in a relaxed environment and receive counselling, if necessary; to reopen the snack bar; to run an advice centre; childcare facilities; a gift shop; a charity shop; a Christian book shop, and so on. The survey had shown that there was a desperate need for childcare in the area, and Census data confirmed that this part of the city had the highest proportion of young children in it – one of the highest proportions in the country. We eventually gave up on all the other ideas and approached a Christian childcare agency (Spurgeons' Child Care) to see if they would work with the Gilgal Project in the downstairs units.

A decision was also needed about what kind of accommodation to offer upstairs. Maria and I went to seek advice from a large Christian housing project in Birmingham, St. Basil's, to see where there was the most need; we visited three projects for women and were told that there was a great shortage of short-term emergency accommodation for women with children.

So finally, the architect drew up plans for a family centre downstairs, offering childcare support in two of the shop units, with a small refuge upstairs, offering secure accommodation for eight women (and their children) who were fleeing domestic violence; it was to have a sleeping-in room, so that 24-hour staff cover would be available. This decision, which I had no particular influence over, was a particular blessing to me, as nearly thirty years before, I had been a victim of domestic violence myself, at a time when there were no refuges to flee to and very few childcare facilities available for the children of lone parents. The steering group decisions about these uses also complied with the words of knowledge given separately to Maria and myself that the buildings would be used for women in need, some of whom would have children.

The steering group also decided that the third shop unit would be rented out commercially to cover the cost of a rental agreement with the housing association, as they owned these units, having bought the whole building for us.

Contracts were signed, the plans approved and the building work put out to tender. The total cost of the refurbishments was of the order of £280,000 – all of this to be found through the partnership with the housing association. God indeed had provided for the vision to be fulfilled. The builders moved in during autumn 1993. There was so much relief within the two fellowships that this point had been reached that a combined praise and prayer meeting was called for one Sunday morning, after the normal morning services. This was held on the pavement outside the buildings.

THE TWO FELLOWSHIPS COMBINE TO PRAISE GOD ON THE PAVEMENT OUTSIDE THE BUILDING

As the building work proceeded, Maurice, one of the steering committee members from the other fellowship, took before and after photographs, as well as a video of the refurbishments and I had the amazing experience of seeing the new tiles go onto the roof, just as in the picture God had given me during the deacon's prayer day. For obvious reasons, we are only able to show the rear of the building in these photographs.

STARTING THE CLEAR-UP PROCESS

BURNING ACCUMULATED RUBBISH IN THE BACK

THE INSIDE OF THE BUILDING BEFORE IT WAS REFURBISHED

WORK NOW BEGINNING INSIDE

WORK BEGINS ON THE SHOP UNITS

WORK BEGINS ON THE ROOFS

NOW NEW ROOF TILES GO ON

THE BUILDING GETS A COAT OF PAINT

THE BEDROOMS ARE PREPARED FOR OCCUPATION

Management agreements were drawn up with the housing association and with Spurgeon's Child Care, who would help to run the family centre. A registered charity and a charitable company were also set up. About this time, a donation of £10,000 towards the furniture needed in the refuge was made available to the project from city council slippage funds. Although the building work had not been completed and we had nowhere to put the furniture, it was bought in faith and placed in storage until the right moment. This turned out to be another miracle of God's provision – a window of opportunity that opened at the right time. That particular city council officer moved on to another post only a week after the donation had been arranged and was later impossible to contact, to thank him for his help. This window of opportunity had happened with the housing association funds and now with the city council funds. God's timing was perfect!

Advertisements were placed for a Manager and staff for the refuge. The first Manager, Nasreen Qureshi, began work on April 5th 1994 and the first residents of the refuge moved in by September of that year. Nasreen had the creative idea of placing the names of women from the Bible on the bedroom doors, rather than using room numbers; these are the names she chose:

Tabitha, Hannah, Leah, Naomi, Priscilla, Ruth, Eunice and Bernice.

Nasreen left eighteen months later, to get married and start a family, and Lynda English, who is still the manager of the refuge today, replaced her.

All of the initial staff were Christian women, who felt called to this work but only one of them had previous experience in a refuge. One was a member of the Oasis team who had done the community research and she is still a member of the staff team. All of the staff quickly gained the skills and sensitivity they needed for the job and most stayed working at the refuge for several years.

Ever since it has opened, the refuge has had virtually 100% occupancy and several women have come to faith during their stay there, by attending our nearby church. One has been baptised and several have had their children dedicated in the church. The running costs of the refuge were initially covered through housing benefit (though now through Supporting People) and this created a dilemma for one woman, who desperately needed a safe place to stay, but she was not eligible to claim benefits. However, a decision was taken by the management committee of the refuge that she was just the kind of person whom the refuge was set up for and so she was offered a place, despite there being no funding to cover the costs of herself and her two children. Amazingly, the money was found and she was later to become a staff member of the Jericho Project and a regular attendee at the church. Her story is told later.

Because it is a refuge, its location has to be kept secret but the police soon began to use it to give training to the Police Domestic Violence Unit, and some of the residents participated in this training. One day, Bill was in the refuge office and a new resident had just arrived. She said that the City authorities had told her she was very lucky to be getting a room at Gilgal. This surprised her, as she was in the process of getting out of a very violent relationship; her only possessions were in a plastic bag and she knew she was going to live in a place of which she had never heard. She asked why she was lucky and the city official told her that she was going to stay in the best refuge in the city. In addition, she was lucky because, only hours earlier, this refuge had had no vacancies. All this within months of it opening! The police also picked up on this and were soon regarding it as the best women's refuge in the city. I believe this happened because God, as part of his "desert will rejoice" proclamation, inspired it.

Now, nine years into its existence, the refuge has secure funding, as well as additional staff to work with the babies and children. The current staff team includes nine people, some of whom are cover workers, to ensure that the refuge is staffed during nights, holidays and weekends; three volunteers also help with the work. The present manager, Lynda English has been with the project since 1996 and has been able to tell us that, since the refuge first opened, 422 women have been accommodated there, with an average of 46 women per year. In 1997-8, changes were made to the refuge due to high demands to accommodate women with children; more of the rooms were turned into family rooms and, as a result, last year more children were accommodated than women. Since 1998, on average there have been 42 children per year staying at the hostel. This led to the need to take on extra staff to work with the children, whilst their mothers were being supported in other ways. Thanks to grants from various generous agencies and trusts, the refuge now has two children's workers attached to the project. There are also plans now to extend the premises at the back, so that additional bedrooms, disabled facilities, play rooms and office space might be added.

Lynda has produced a little booklet, which describes the work of the refuge. The majority of it is reproduced in the following text boxes:

WHAT IS GILGAL?

Gilgal is a refuge for women and their dependent children who are homeless as a result of domestic violence. The refuge offers safe accommodation at a confidential address and accepts and admits referrals 24 hours a day. Referrals are accepted from any agency or any individual, including self-referrals.

The refuge is staffed at all times 365 days a year and there are no exceptions. Gilgal staff are on duty at the refuge at all times, including overnights, weekends and public holidays, to ensure the residents needs are met, maximise the security of the refuge and to deal with any emergency or admission which may occur out of hours...

The rooms are prepared in advance. As soon as a room becomes vacant, it is cleaned and made ready for the next occupant. Rooms have all usual bedroom furniture, a hand washbasin and a vanity unit. Beds are made up and fresh towels and toiletries put into the room, so women and children have all essentials, no matter how little they bring with them. The Children's Workers also put appropriate toys and a welcome pack in each room, as soon as we know how many children will be living there and their ages. Every child's bed always has a teddy or similar soft toy sitting on the pillow ready to welcome a new child, who may not have been able to bring a bedtime friend with them. These things will never replace the things they have had to leave behind, but will sometimes fill a gap at a traumatic time in their lives.

On arrival, the woman and her child or children are made welcome, offered a drink and formally admitted to the refuge by the worker on duty. She will be shown her room and introduced to any other residents who are in the building. Workers always check if the woman needs medical attention and if she has food or money to buy food...

WHAT IS GILGAL (contd.)?

Accommodation at Gilgal is not self-contained. Residents have their own bedrooms, which are lockable, but, apart from this, every other facility is shared. Eight women and their children share a kitchen, dining room, lounge, bathrooms, toilets, showers and laundry. Predictably, there are occasionally disagreements but, on the whole, women cope extremely well with shared facilities and the plus factor is that women do not become isolated. Although it can be difficult for a person newly moved in to adjust to communal living, there are people around to welcome and support new residents, which would not happen in self-contained accommodation. There is always someone to put a kettle on, hold a baby, or help carry belongings to a room.

All shared areas of the house are fully equipped with furniture, appliances and equipment. There is a private, secure garden at the rear of the house, which is well equipped with outdoor play equipment for the resident children. In addition, there is a large play cabin where children's indoor activities take place.

The Refuge Project Workers support women throughout their stay at Gilgal, networking with a wide range of professionals, to ensure that all needs are met.... Women and children have Individual Support plans, which are drawn up in partnership with their named worker. All people have differing needs, so at Gilgal we aim to treat everyone as an individual and provide support tailored to each person's perceived need. Women and children have a one to one time with their named worker – this is a time to explore issues, ask for help, plan for the future, discuss any concerns....

Many women lack confidence to such a degree that they believe they are not competent to carry out even simple tasks. Many have been told they are useless repeatedly until it becomes a way of life and they believe it. It takes time, and a great deal of encouragement, to overcome this and it is part of the work that all staff at Gilgal undertake every day.

WHAT IS GILGAL (contd.)?

Women and children develop close friendships within the refuge, which often continue after they leave Gilgal. Although the staff provide much support to the residents, we must never underestimate how much support the women give to each other. No matter how little they may have, women can always find something to give to each other. They offer each other emotional support and practical assistance.

The refuge is a very nurturing environment. Women begin to heal and believe in themselves. They have freedom of choice and friends, both of which are new experiences for women who have lived with a violent and abusive partner. Children too thrive in the communal, family-style environment. We watch individuals of all ages grow in confidence and prepare themselves to move on.

We do our utmost during people's stay at Gilgal to support without creating dependency. Our aim is to equip women with skills to enable them to move on in confidence and take their rightful place back in the community. Refuge staff assist women to obtain grants and furniture to equip their new homes. We also offer some short-term support after a family moves out of the refuge. Not all women want this but the majority do. As pleased as they are to be re-housed in their own accommodation, they are often a little scared of going out into the world on their own.... Children's workers, too, offer a similar service to ensure children's needs are not forgotten...

U's STORY

I came to the UK during the 1990's with my husband, who is a professional man, and my son. My daughter was born in 1996 and domestic violence started towards me about a year after this, after my husband returned from a visit overseas. I had to suffer both verbal and physical abuse in the home and I was also slapped on the face whilst out shopping with my husband. I became very depressed.

My son encouraged me to seek help and I was interviewed by a member of the staff at Gilgal on a Friday during 1998. The staff were very friendly but could not help me that day; however, they showed me a room at the refuge and said they would try to work something out for me by Monday. They kept their word and the Refuge Manager and another woman who eventually became my Project Worker interviewed me again on the Monday; I told them about what had been happening to me. They phoned Social Services and the benefit office but found that I was not entitled to any benefits if I left my husband. In such circumstances the refuge would not be able to offer me a place, but the Manager told me not to worry and she spoke to the Chairman of the project, who agreed to take me on as an exceptional case. They offered me a place at the refuge, with my son (then aged 13-14 years) and my daughter and I stayed there for 10 months.

U's STORY (Contd)

During that time, the staff helped to build up my confidence and helped me with finances; they were very friendly and supportive. They also introduced me to the nearby Baptist Church, where I made other new friends, who were also supportive to me, and I still have these people as friends. I was able to find somewhere else to live and moved out of the refuge in March 1999. A community worker also helped me to find part-time work with Stepping Stones and then another person at the church helped me to get a full-time job at the Jericho Project, where I was also given help to get a nursery placement for my daughter.

I have now become a new woman, able to stand on my own feet. In February 2000, I was offered a permanent job with the Jericho Community Business. I still keep in touch with the Gilgal refuge and often visit there, especially for their Christmas parties. If it were not for Gilgal, and the people at the church, I don't know what I would have done.

The family centre opened downstairs a few months after the refuge, in January 1995, and was named "Stepping Stones" – after the twelve stones that were taken from the bed of the River Jordan, as the people of Israel crossed on dry land, and used them to build a monument at Gilgal (Joshua 4:19-24), to remind them of the miracle that God had wrought in opening up the river before them.

It was good that this part of the project could be developed in conjunction with a Christian childcare agency, Spurgeon's, who provided a large proportion of the finances needed for the work at this early stage. The first manager of Stepping Stones, Val Floy, was employed by Spurgeon's Child Care; their expertise in staffing and policy issues was to be invaluable to the project. Val developed a number of facilities for the children of the area, and the place was always a hive of busy and happy activity. After a few years in the job, Val was promoted to a regional role within Spurgeon's Child Care and her place at Stepping Stones was taken over by Margaret Morcom. The project soon outgrew the available space in the shop units, so that other projects have now begun in schools and community centres up and down the main road and then in other parts of the city. Now, eight years into the project, it has become a professional service, supported by statutory agencies and Barnardo's, as well as Spurgeon's Child Care. A leaflet has been produced (and is extracted in the text boxes following), which describes each facet of the work.

STEPPING STONES

PRE-SCHOOL GROUP

The Pre-School group is registered with Social Services to take twenty children aged two and a half to five years per session. The children are arranged into key groups with trained, qualified staff with a high adult: child ratio. There is a curriculum, which is geared to meet individual children's needs.

The group receives OFSTED inspections, which validate its educational provision. The group is registered to receive the Nursery Grant for children aged 3-4 years from the Education Dept.

There is a waiting list for children; it is recommended that children's names are put on a list to secure a place.

Participation of parents is welcomed via the parent's rota – new parents are welcome to come and visit the Group.

STAY AND PLAY

The Stay and Play group is for parents and carers to bring their children, aged 0-4 years. It offers opportunity:
- To make new friends
- Time to talk with other parents
- To allow children to mix and enjoy play activities
- Refreshments and drinks
- First stage for children before Pre-School

The sessions are informal and flexible. There are always staff on hand to welcome new members of the group and to help children to play and mix with other children. There is no need to book. Just turn up for the sessions as you wish.

STEPPING STONES ACTIVITIES (contd)

FAMILY SUPPORT

Family support work is part of our home support service and is carried out by family support workers. The work is mainly at crisis level although preventative work is also undertaken.

We will support parents who have children up to the age of 16 years, who live with them at least part of the week. Other agencies may refer into the service and we also take self-referrals for families in our catchment area.

We can assist with issues such as:
- Managing children's behaviour
- Domestic violence
- Parenting issues

while taking into account other influential issues, such as debt, housing, disability and health.

HOME SUPPORT SERVICE

This is co-ordinated by our family support workers. The Home Support Workers are fully trained, supervised and authorized volunteers who can offer support if you:
- Feel isolated at home
- Need some help coping with your child
- Need someone who will listen to you
- Need advice

Home support workers can also accompany parents to court, solicitors or hospital. Families must live in our catchment area.

WOMEN'S GROUP

This group is open to all women whether or not they have children under 5. It is an opportunity for time away from the children to talk, make friends and have a breather. The sessions are friendly, informal and informative, covering subjects like relaxation, assertiveness, personal safety, health issues, children's development, and women's issues. Crèche provision is available for children aged 0-5, if required.

Initially, the Stepping Stones' work was to help families in need living in the immediate vicinity, with the pre-school group and "stay and play" groups for parents and children. Val increased the staff team, with the help of grants, and recruited volunteers, so that work was able to start out in the community, with home support workers. Workshops were also begun in parenting skills and play, as well as training courses in Child Care, run in conjunction with colleges of higher education. Stepping Stones soon outgrew the available space and so the office moved to the church itself and work began in local schools. Margaret started to expand the work in the local community and the staff team increased to 24 paid workers, with 16 volunteers. Two more initiatives, recently begun are "The Arch Project" – an early intervention service for children, aged 5-13 years with emotional and behavioural needs, and their parents; and STEP2, a project which works with young people aged 5-13 years, at risk of social exclusion, to build self esteem and confidence and to improve physical, social and mental health, educational performance and emotional resilience, so as to reduce the risks of bullying, truancy and crime.

Some of the parents and children who have been helped by Stepping Stones have attended our nearby church and Sunday School. Every so often, a special service is held at the church to share how the work is going and some of the people who have been helped by Stepping Stones tell their stories. The following text box gives a few excerpts of people's stories.

STEPPING STONES FAMILY SUPPORT PROJECT – A PLACE OF NEW BEGINNINGS – COMMENTS FROM SERVICE USERS

"I wish I had known about you earlier. At last someone is there who can help me look to the future, who answers my questions instead of saying, 'I can't help'."
[Mother of a baby daughter with multiple disabilities]

"Just from this one visit I feel so much better. It's as if my life has been turned around. I'm not alone any more."
[Very young lone mother who had been disowned by her family]

"We don't want to go to court, but if you are with us, we can do it."
[Young parents with learning difficulties, who had been victims of deception and fraud]

"You have helped me so much and I find having you spend so much time with me something has rubbed off. I have started praying and thinking more about God." [Mother of traumatized children]

"I must be happy. I keep coming back to Stepping Stones. I have been coming for over two years now. My child has been through Stay and Play, as well as pre-School. She leaves in July to go to Reception Class in September but I will be coming to the Holiday Club and Stay and Play until she leaves. We have moved house now but I still bring her here. [Mother]

"I had a list of six agencies I'd found in the phone book. The first five said they couldn't help. When you answered the phone and said 'Yes', I couldn't talk. I put down the phone and cried." [Mother of a teenage boy with many problems]

The whole Gilgal project has now been going for almost ten years and, during this time, another miracle happened. I was unaware of the fact that Bill was quite worried about the terms of the tenancy agreement for the shop units that we had with the housing association, who had encouraged us not to buy outright. If ownership remained with them, they would be responsible for the cost of maintenance and repairs. The original agreement was for us to pay a low rental for five years, after which time, a full commercial rent would have to be paid. During the first five years, we were able to cover these costs by renting out one unit to a travel agent. However, this was fraught with all kinds of problems, not the least of which was actually getting the money paid on time. Then the travel agent moved out and a decision had to be made about whether to find another tenant. All of this happened, in addition to needing to find increased amounts to pay the housing association after five years.

Bill told me about a wonderful revelation he had had earlier from God during 1992, which was a reassurance to him that all the funds would be provided for the Gilgal Project. He had been travelling back by car from a ministers' retreat in Cambridgeshire, as a front seat passenger. During the journey, there was a storm and Bill had looked out of the window to see the end of a rainbow touching the ground. At the same time, he heard God speaking to him, with the following words:

"*All that I have promised I will do, I will do!*"

He believed the rainbow to be a sign from God to reinforce the promise in these words. But this promise was not to be completely fulfilled for another four years, when an acquaintance of Bill who lived in Bristol, suddenly died. This woman had been receiving church newsletters and progress reports about the Gilgal Project and knew all about it. To Bill's amazement, she had left the Gilgal project £100,000 in her will "*to ensure that we could obtain the leasehold of the premises*". Bill was able to use the legacy to pay off the housing association debt, so that no further rental for the shop units was required. A legally binding agreement was drawn up to this effect. The surprising thing about this was God's timing again. He did not provide the money earlier but just at the point when it was needed, when the rents were due to increase substantially. And, as a result, Eileen's picture of golden bank notes and Bill's rainbow promise both turned out to be extremely accurate prophetic signs about this work.

The Gilgal and Stepping Stones ministries are a demonstration of God's unconditional love that he has especially for people in need. Many of the people helped by this project have been rejected by others and damaged by them but, coming to the refuge and Stepping Stones has helped them to experience something of God's unconditional love, as expressed through his servants working with each of the projects. The other picture that Eileen received, way back at the beginning of God's revelations about the project – of Jesus going amongst a crowd of people on the streets of the city, touching them and healing them – has indeed also become a reality. Many people (and children too) have already been healed emotionally as a result of the work.

And John's picture about the airport lounge has also come to fulfilment. Several of the people in the church are now involved in this ministry to the multi-ethnic population of this part of Birmingham's inner city; some as staff or volunteers (indeed, John himself has played a grandfatherly role to many of the children who have come to the project), others through the management committees and others through financial support. So many people have now played a part in the work that it is impossible to name them all!

Bill retired as minister of the church in 1999 and then began an international ministry, visiting churches all over the world. He has shared the story of Gilgal with people in California, in Siberia, in Malawi and in the Middle East. The message about it has also reached India, through a Christian magazine. In each of these countries, this story has inspired Christians to have confidence in hearing God's word and acting on it. We do hope that, now the story is written down, it will have a similar effect in encouraging Christians throughout the UK and elsewhere, to listen to God, to act on his word and to have faith that he will provide the means to work out his purposes in this world.

As I write this story, in September 2003, we have just had a celebration of the whole Gilgal Project. It is now 10 years since the builders first moved in to start repairing the derelict buildings. In that time, so much has happened and the two elements of the project have expanded so much, that it is time for them to split into two separate charities in their own right. The refuge now employs nine staff and has three volunteers; it receives referrals from all over the country. Stepping Stones now works also in the north and east of Birmingham, in partnership with Barnardo's as well as Spurgeons's Child Care, and employs 24 staff and 16 volunteers. Through God's grace, the work has expanded so much. When God first spoke to us, we would never have believed how much he would do through this derelict building and the two projects there. What a privilege to have been involved in its setting up!

"Then to Lord said to Moses, 'Is there any limit to my power? Now you will see whether or not my word comes true'."
Numbers 11:23 (NLT)

CHAPTER TWO

Reversals!

In the previous chapter, I mentioned the spiritual concept of "reversals". I believe this to be an important factor affecting most of God's major plans for his Kingdom, here on earth. I will therefore examine the concept in more detail, as reversals have played their part at every stage of the three-part revelation of God's plans for the Gilgal, Jericho and Bethel projects.

During the development of the Gilgal Project, we were experiencing many blockages, delays and problems, as we tried to take forward the vision. At one point (when it appeared that Mr R. had bought the derelict buildings), it seemed like we had lost the project altogether and most of the people involved began to wonder whether we had got it all wrong.

During this period, I went to visit my elderly mother in Berkshire. I had been sharing with my parents over the months the ups and downs of the Gilgal project and Mum therefore knew of the problems we had been experiencing. During my visit, she eagerly thrust some Bible reading notes into my hand.

"This will help you to understand your difficulties with Gilgal at the moment," she told me.

I took the notes home and studied them. They were from an "Every Day With Jesus" series, published by CWR in Sept/Oct 1987 and written by Selwyn Hughes, with a further study section by Trevor J. Partridge. Mum must have had them in her possession for three years before passing them on to me but she was right about the notes, as their message was spot on for our situation at that time.

With permission from CWR, I now quote extensively from these Bible notes, as they are relevant for, not only the progress of Gilgal, but also of Jericho and Bethel. I also believe that these insights will help to anyone else who is led by God into developing new work for him.

The notes describe the ways in which God works and discuss situations in which everything seems to go wrong, from a human perspective. Selwyn Hughes encourages the reader to see things from God's point of view when this happens. He writes as follows:

"You would think that if God loved us so much as He says He does, He would lead us, not into troublesome situations but away from them... At such times we cry out: Why is God allowing this to happen to me? How can God say He loves me when He fails to answer my prayers and deliver me from such dark and difficult situations... It may appear on the surface of things that the Almighty has lost control – but nothing could be further from the truth. God never loses control of anything. If you could penetrate the depths of the divine heart, you would see a purpose being worked out that would more than compensate for your feelings of uncertainty and doubt..."

In his notes for Saturday 19th September 1987, in a section entitled "Reasons for Reversals", are the following words:

"It is now time to ask the question: why does God adopt these strange and mysterious methods of working? He does it, not because he likes to tantalise us or play games, but because there is just no other way that he can bring about his perfect purposes.

"You see, when God reveals something to us, He knows that at the moment of some fresh unfolding of His will, we have within us a combination of godly concerns and human perspectives. We are eager, alert and full of natural enthusiasm. He knows that our natural enthusiasm is the thing that helps us get going to do His bidding, but a moment has to come when our natural enthusiasm is overlaid by divine perspectives.

How does God achieve this? He allows us to go ahead in the strength of our own eagerness and then, at the appropriate moment, He changes gear and puts things into reverse. When we come to this point, we realise that if the revelation that God has given us is to be realised, then it will not be because of our strength and prowess – but His.

When we learn that lesson, then God miraculously intervenes to restore His purposes. Note the word 'miraculously'. The fact that things are restored miraculously is then a constant reminder that God must always have the biggest part in a project. In that way, no onlooker can be in doubt as to who is responsible – everyone recognises it to be God."

In telling the story of the Gilgal Project, you will note that I used the word "miraculous" on several occasions. This is because, to all the people involved in the project at that time, it really felt as if miracles were happening: the fact that the revelation was given to two women independently, who had never met each other before; the agreement of the owner to sell the derelict premises, after years of deliberation, exactly at the time when the housing association had spare funds; the provision of funds to buy and refurbish the premises at exactly the right moment; the willingness of Christian people (including pensioners) to sacrificially offer their life savings to the project, after an earlier time of scepticism; the legacy given to the project five years on, at exactly the moment when the rent for the shop units were due for increase. All these were miracles. And for Jericho, a similar list could be made. And, because of all these miracles, it is fitting that the Lord revealed to Maria Blom that the name for the project should be Gilgal, after the monument that was built to remind the Israelites of the miraculous crossing of the River Jordan.

The Bible reading notes examine whether God follows the same pattern with all his revelations and conclude that this is not always the case – but it most certainly is for God's major revelations. The notes describe the acquisition of Waverley Abbey House as a base for CWR's teaching and training work, which followed a similar pattern of reversals. The point is made that the biographies of great Christian leaders and the histories of famous Christian movements show that, invariably, God revealed his purposes to them and then put things into reverse:

"Then, at an appropriate moment and in His own good time, He restored the original revelation in a miraculous and supernatural manner."

The notes suggest that a similar pattern was present in the Bible, especially during the ministry of Jesus. He announced that he was in the world to establish the Kingdom of God and had multitudes responding to his message and seeing the miracles he performed. Yet this all went into reverse at his crucifixion:

"The revelation Christ had given concerning the Kingdom of God was seemingly at a point where it could never be restored. Whoever survived a crucifixion? But three days after His death on the cross, God miraculously raised Him from the dead and restored to the dispirited Peter, as well as the rest of the disciples, the truth that had first laid siege to their hearts."

The Bible is full of other examples of God's power at work in this way. After the wonderful revelations accompanying the birth of Jesus in a stable in Bethlehem, announcing that he was the expected Messiah, his parents had to flee for their lives to Egypt. Other examples in the Old Testament are: the story of Joseph, in which he had amazing dreams (revelations) about his future role, only to be sold into slavery in Egypt; the pursuit of David by the jealous Saul, after he had been anointed as future king by Samuel and had slain Goliath in a miraculous way; the story of the rebuilding of the temple by Nehemiah (which had several reversals, when Sanballat and his group tried to stop the work); the rescue of Shadrach, Meshach and Abednego from the burning, fiery furnace and the miracle of Daniel being thrown into the lion's den but being untouched by the lions. All of these are examples of God saving and using his people in miraculous ways, to further his kingdom on earth, to strengthen the faith of his followers and to witness to his power to non-believers.

I believe that God used the same principle through the Gilgal Project, which underwent four reversals, and also through the Jericho Project (described in the next chapter), which underwent five reversals. Out of Jericho, a new project is being developed for former drug addicts and homeless people (called Project Renaissance-21), which has already experienced its first reversal (a major secular funding body pulled out and it seemed as if the project could not go ahead, then a Christian businessman offered to make up the difference). The third part of Maria Blom's prophecy indicated a project to be called Bethel. Chapter 4 will describe the revelation associated with Bethel, which is also currently in reversal.

And the projects, once they have got off the ground, are still not immune from difficulties. Our experience with Gilgal, Stepping Stones and Jericho has demonstrated that their managers become targets for attack by the evil one. The projects survive because God inspired the work but we must be constantly vigilant in the prayer support of their leaders, if the work is to continue.

CHAPTER THREE

Jericho!

*"I will turn the darkness into light before them
and make the rough places smooth."*
Isaiah 42:16 (NIV)

The Jericho vision started about the same time as that of Gilgal though, at that early stage, it was not given a particular name. The vision-holder for this project was Rev. John Mallard, pastor of another inner city Baptist church, Edward Road Baptist Church in Balsall Heath. John had been running a drop-in centre in the church hall there every Wednesday for 20 years, when I first met him in 1987. He ran it with another Christian, Tom Stinchcombe, and groups of unemployed men came there to play snooker, have a free cup of coffee and a chat. The church was located in a multi-ethnic, multi-faith area, with many multi-occupied dwellings, high unemployment, as well as problems of drug dealing, mugging and prostitution. John has a wonderful heart of love for all people and especially for people who have difficulties in their lives. His whole ministry at the church was characterised by this loving spirit, which I believe to be a special anointing from God.

As well as helping John to run the drop-in centre, Tom had begun a ministry amongst the prostitutes of the area, called COGS (Christian Outreach to Girls on the Streets), in which teams of people went out after dark with hot soup, offering to pray for the women, whilst they stood on street corners. Several of the women had given their hearts to the Lord, some had left prostitution and one or two had been baptised.

When I first went to visit the drop-in centre, John and Tom shared with me that they would like to offer more than just a drop-in for the unemployed; they both had skills that they had acquired during their working lives in industry and they wanted to share these skills with the men, by setting up a training centre. John shared with me his vision for such a training centre.

Not long before this, a number of pastors and members of the inner city Baptist churches had visited a project in Plaistow, in the East End of London, which was a large building project, offering flats (accommodation) for the homeless, a drop-in facility with jobsearch for the unemployed and a café, with cheap, nutritious meals. I talked to John about the London project and we decided to use it as a model for Balsall Heath. Together we planned a project containing a raft of facilities for the needy people of the area. As well as the training centre, there would be a crèche, for the children of lone parents using the centre, a hostel for homeless people and a café (or community restaurant), serving cheap, nutritious meals to the local community, which would also act as a place where the courses in the training centre would be advertised, thus providing a bridge to encourage people who would not normally attend an educational establishment. It would give them confidence to taste what was on offer in the training centre. It was anticipated that the main client group would be the unemployed, of whom some would be ex-offenders and others might have drug- or alcohol-related problems, as well as young single people with housing need. The centre might also be used to help rehabilitate some of the women who were being contacted through the COGS project, helping them to exit prostitution.

We looked for an empty site near the church where a training centre might be built and, to our surprise, were directed by City Council planners to a site just opposite the church. It was located on one side of a triangle of streets, right in the middle of the red light district of the city. Two of the streets in the triangle consisted of terraced houses, backing onto one another; none of these houses had front gardens and many of them were therefore used for prostitution. Women would sit, scantily-clad in the front windows, touting for business at all hours of the day and night; other, younger women controlled by pimps, would solicit from nearby street corners in all kinds of inclement weather.

This empty site seemed and ideal place to develop Christian ministry in the area but, as with the Gilgal Project, there was no money to buy the land, nor to develop a new centre. A committee of church members and other relevant people was set up to manage and develop the project. Most of the church members were from the West Indian community and provided a valuable rooting for the work within the local community. Discussions were started with a housing association (a different one from Gilgal), who agreed to purchase the land and to work in partnership with the church. Application was also made to the Inner City Partnership Programme (a mixture of national and local funds). A local college agreed to be involved in the development of the training centre and a development officer, Alan Harris, was appointed to get the project off the ground. Jane Gallagher followed him in this role in 1995.

An architect drew up plans, which included warden-controlled flats for homeless people, a training centre, a crèche and a café. Unfortunately, when the plans went out to consultation, during the planning approval process, people in the local community completely disapproved of them, especially of the café, as they feared it would be used by drug dealers and would encourage prostitution. Because of its work helping women to exit from prostitution, through the COGS project, the church already had a reputation locally; it was perceived as condoning and encouraging prostitution, which was far from the case. We did not realise at that stage that a whispering campaign of false rumours was already being conducted against the church and this project.

A public meeting was called in the church hall, to try to allay some of these fears, but it was attended by scores of vindictive people, who shouted, abused and accused and failed to listen to the truth. This was a very low period during the development of the work – the time of its first reversal.

About this time, a small group of people started meeting early in the morning, and then on Wednesday lunchtimes, to pray about the vision and to seek confirmation that it was of the Lord. A number of Bible passages and pictures were received, all of which were an encouragement to proceed with the work needed to set up the project and to have confidence that God was behind it (Isaiah 41:10: 1 Chronicles 2:14-16; Luke 11:9-10; Neh. 2:17-

20). The prayer group began to go out prayer walking in the area every week, particularly concentrating on the triangle of streets surrounding the site we had been offered. Two Asian Christians, Salim and Shamim Stephen, joined this prayer walking group, as well as others from the management committee of the project (David and Janet Harmer), Pearl Barnes from the church and others from neighbouring churches, who came from time to time. The prayer walk, of course, also passed the women who were touting for business from their windows and sometimes people from the group would stop and pray for them individually – the women would often share with members of the group the difficulties they had in their lives and gave information about things that were happening locally. The prayer walk also went right past the empty land, so the group sometimes stopped and claimed it for the Lord, placing a cross there as part of a symbolic action. It was because of this circular prayer walk that the project eventually became called "The Jericho Community Project", after the story in Joshua 6:

> *"Then the Lord said to Joshua, 'See, I have delivered Jericho into your hands, along with its king and its fighting men. March around the city once with all the armed men. Do this for six days. Make seven priests carry trumpets of rams' horns in front of the ark. On the seventh day, march around the city seven times, with the priests blowing the trumpets. When you hear them sound a long blast on the trumpets, make all the people give a loud shout; then the wall of the city will collapse and the people will go up, every man straight in'..."*
> Joshua 6: 2-5 (NIV) then following for rest of story

JANE AND PEARL PRAYER WALKING IN THE RAIN

The prayer walk around the triangle of streets continued weekly for several years (rather than the 7 days in the Bible story), until the project eventually got off the ground. In the intervening years a number of things happened, which will be described in detail, as they are relevant to the whole story.

In the early days because of local opposition and a reluctance to support the work by statutory officials, there was so little movement forward in the project that a special prayer meeting was called, to check that the vision was of the Lord and to seek the way forward. On the evening it was arranged, several of the prayer group became ill and so, only two people actually attended – the pastor, John, and myself. Nevertheless, the moment we started to pray, a powerful thing happened. Both of us independently saw a brilliant light, which lit up the whole area, like a beacon. This was an unmistakable confirmation to us that the vision was of the Lord and that we should persevere in trying to get it off the ground. During this prayer meeting, the Lord also led us to a particular passage of scripture (Revelation 12), which describes the battle between good and evil (between God and Satan) and of the final victory of the Lord, achieved through the death of his son and the shedding of his blood on the cross:

> *"And there was war in heaven. Michael and his angels fought against the dragon, and the dragon and his angels fought back. But he was not strong enough, and they lost their place in heaven. The great dragon was hurled down – that ancient serpent called the devil, or Satan, who leads the whole world astray. He was hurled to earth and his angels with him...*
>
> *They overcame him with the blood of the Lamb and by the word of their testimony; they did not love their lives so much as to shrink from death....... Then the dragon was enraged at the woman and went off to make war against the rest of her offspring – those who obey God's commandments and hold to the testimony of Jesus."*
> Rev. 12: 7-11 (NIV)

This passage helped us to see that the opposition to the project that had been received was Satanic in origin and that, indeed, we would be facing much spiritual warfare in the setting up this Christian project. We were encouraged to keep going.

THIS IS ME, SITTING ON THE WALL OUTSIDE THE CHURCH WITH SALIM AND SHAMIM STEPHEN. BEHIND US IS REV. JOHN MALLARD, THE VISIONARY FOR THE PROJECT

Over the next few months, some strange but significant facts were discovered about that triangle of streets. By now, I was working full time in the community as an employee of the Jericho Community Project. I had felt called to offer a ministry of love to the people in the Balsall Heath community and had become involved in outreach work and in running the drop-in centre, which began to offer specific job search support. By now, most of the people seeking help from the drop-in were young men, particularly from the Pakistani and Yemeni communities. Amongst these was a small group of Pakistani teenagers, who came regularly to use the drop-in facilities but who had problems with drugs' misuse; contact with them was to be extremely challenging over the next few years.

Through local contacts I learnt that, not only were the streets a centre for prostitution and drug dealing, but there was a gambling den and several people living in these streets were involved in witchcraft or voodoo; there were at least three people in those streets who were involved in witchcraft and 20 covens in that part of the city. Some of these facts were learnt from the prostitutes themselves; one of them was very much involved in the occult and offered a potion or a charm to the other women for just about every eventuality that might occur in their lives.

One day, I was praying in the area alone, when I felt the Lord guide me to the home of one of the men, B, who had been most vindictive at the public meeting – he was an aggressive man, full of hate and anger. I was afraid to visit him but I knew the Lord wanted me to go and would therefore protect me, so I took a copy of our architectural plans for the site with me and knocked on his door. B invited me in and I showed him the plans, saying to him,

"We believe that this training centre and café will happen because God has inspired it."

Before I had hardly finished the sentence, B's face changed and he snarled at me, "I don't believe in God! I'm a Wiccan!

As long as I live here, I will make sure that your project will never get off the ground!"

I was shocked by his attitude and words and hastily made my retreat, hoping that the Lord had just wanted us to learn this piece of information from the visit. I did not know what a wiccan was then but later found out that wicca is a form of witchcraft, based on nature – a religion that had its roots in pre-Christian times. This man was a witch!

Witches from this sect belong to covens, usually comprised of 13 people and, contrary to popular belief, men are very much a part of these covens. Wicca has many rituals – for initiation, healing and protection, as well as rituals for the sun and the sea. Most witches practice clairvoyance and divination, using tarot cards, crystal balls and black mirrors. It is possible that the prostitute offering potions and charms, who lived just along the road from him, was another member of his coven.

Learning this about B gave us an opportunity to pray for him in a specific way. I had read somewhere that praying for people who are involved in the occult in the name of Jesus can release them from it, so this is what we did. Not many months after this, B left the area and set up home in another part of the city; we don't know whether he was released from witchcraft, but his influence in Balsall Heath was removed.

Another day, one of the women sitting soliciting from her window, C, called me in for a chat. I sat on the bed in the front room of this small back-to-back terrace. Apart from the bed and a chair and TV, the room was bare. A friend of hers, D, was making up her face and arranging her hair in preparation for her later activities. C knew I was a Christian and made a strange remark to me, with a smirk,

"If you carried a cross around this area, it would sizzle!"

I asked her what she meant by this and she continued vaguely, "All the stuff that goes on around here."

She was referring to the voodoo, witchcraft, black magic, drug pushing, muggings, shootings and other shady activities that were regularly practised in the area. I knew that C herself had been mixed up in some of this (she seemed to be attracted to things that had an element of risk in them), though she was vehemently opposed to drug pushing. I decided to use her comments to remind her of God's love for her.

"But there is a cross here, right in the middle of it all," I said, referring to both the church and to the cross that had been placed on the piece of land, "God has placed his cross right here in Balsall Heath because, through the cross where Jesus died and the blood that he shed on the cross, he can conquer evil. He conquers everything on the darker side as he is more powerful than Satan"

C was very much aware of the struggle between darkness and light that was a part of everyday life in Balsall Heath at that time and which was, indeed, very much a part of her own life struggle.

"You'd be interested in what I witnessed last night as I was sitting in the window," she said, changing the subject. "There was this poor Irishman lying in the gutter, bleeding, and these other guys were kicking him. I think he must have said something that annoyed them, so they were having a go at him, those violent guys who sell the drugs. I was so angry when I saw it that I went outside and pushed right into the middle of them, told them to "F off". Then I helped the Irishman to get up and I brought him in here. I even washed the blood off his face with my best green flannel. When he was feeling a bit better, I found somebody who had a car and got them to take him home."

"You took a risk, C," I said, "But I'm glad you told me that story because there's a story in the Bible just like yours. I read to her the story of the Good Samaritan from St. Luke's gospel, and then left the Bible with her, open at this page, so that she could read the story for herself later, though I knew that her reading skills were poor.

A few days later, C came into the church whilst the group was praying there on a Wednesday. She wanted to tell us that she had been reading the Bible, whilst sitting in the window waiting for clients. "I like St. Luke's gospel the best," she stated. Several months later, she was to tell me that reading this gospel had helped her to come off drugs and that she found she could now control some of her more violent impulses (she previously had a criminal conviction for GBH).

Pearl, one of the church members, had been opening the church on a Wednesday for several years, as she felt that this was what God was calling her to do. She placed a board outside, which simply stated, "This church is open for prayer and meditation."

THE BOARD OUTSIDE THE OPEN DOOR OF THE CHURCH

It was through this board that we had first met C. She had come bursting in one Wednesday, a loud, brash and aggressive woman, but she sat down quietly among us, as we prayed and sang worship songs. We had asked if she wanted us to pray for her and she had nodded. As we lay our hands on her and prayed, the tears had started to trickle down her face. I felt the movement of the Holy Spirit as he brought a picture to share with C. It was a picture of Jesus, holding out his hands to her. This seemed to have significance for her and she continued to weep; she later told me that she had a picture of Jesus, just like this one, in her home. We began to visit her in her home, to offer practical support and to pray for her from time to time. And I believe that it was because of this that she became like Rahab to the Jericho Project; she provided information that helped in claiming the area for the Lord, as well as introducing us to other prostitutes who were in need.

One of these was P, who lived and worked from another terraced house that backed onto where C worked. Janet and I met C in the street one day and she said,

"Come with me. There's something I want to show you!"

She led us to P's house and took us right through into the back garden.

"Look!" she exclaimed, pointing to the back wall of the house. There, painted in colourful life-size dimensions, were two huge satanic images. Janet, my companion, recognised one horned image as Herne the Hunter and there was another one with pigs. We recognised their symbolism immediately and told the two women about this. P's face turned a greenish tinge of white.

"They were there on the house when I first moved in," she muttered. "I heard that the woman who lived here before me was into mirror gazing and stuff like that!"

"I told you what they were but you wouldn't believe me," retorted C.

It was clear that we had come across another manifestation of the Wicca coven in the area. Janet immediately prayed for any evil power to come out of these images and we later exorcised and blessed the house and cleansed it with holy water. The back wall was also whitewashed, to remove the images.

Not long after that P left prostitution. She had not been able to keep up the payments of her mortgage on the house and so she left the house too and moved into a flat a mile away. Did the house cleansing have something to do with P's decision to leave prostitution? She was no longer in the grip of the occultic powers that had been lingering there and so maybe she could begin to think rationally about her future. The house was repossessed and refurbished and is now used for normal residential purposes.

This work amongst the women in prostitution did not go unnoticed by other local residents, who wanted to rid the area completely of prostitution and they saw the Jericho Project's activities as condoning it. Sadly, they were not aware of the following story, to be found in Luke 7: 36-50 (NIV):

> "Now one of the Pharisees invited Jesus to have dinner with him, so he went to the Pharisee's house and reclined at the table. When a woman who had lived a sinful life in that town learned that Jesus was eating at the Pharisee's house, she brought an alabaster jar of perfume, and as she stood behind him at his feet weeping, she began to wet his feet with her tears. Then she wiped them with her hair, kissed them and poured perfume on them.
>
> When the Pharisee who had invited him saw this, he said to himself, 'If this man were a prophet, he would know who is touching him and what kind of woman she is – that she is a sinner.'
>
> Jesus answered him, 'Simon, I have something to tell you.'
>
> 'Tell me teacher,' he said.
>
> 'Two men owed money to a certain money-lender. One owed him five hundred denarii, and the other fifty. Neither of them had the money to pay him back, so he cancelled the debts of both. Now which of them will love him more?'

> Simon replied, 'I suppose the one who had the bigger debt cancelled.'
>
> 'You have judged correctly,' Jesus said.
>
> Then he turned towards the woman and said to Simon, 'Do you see this woman? I came into your house. You did not give me any water for my feet, but she wet my feet with her tears and wiped them with her hair. You did not give me a kiss, but this woman, from the time I entered has not stopped kissing my feet. You did not pour oil on my head, but she has poured perfume on my feet. Therefore, I tell you that her many sins have been forgiven – for she loved much. But he who has been forgiven little, loves little.'
>
> Then Jesus said to her, 'Your sins are forgiven.'
>
> The other guests began to say among themselves, 'Who is this who forgives sins?'
>
> Jesus said to the woman, 'Your faith has saved you. Go in peace.'"
>
> Luke 7: 36-50 (NIV)

I am sure that it is this story that had helped C to decide that she liked St. Luke's gospel the best.

Other things happened that convinced us that the battle between good and evil was still raging in the area. One day, when the church was open for prayer, a Sikh couple came in. They asked for prayer and then described a number of problems that the family had. The wife was constantly ill, though the doctors could find nothing wrong with her, and the husband too had some psychological problems. They said that they had seen unpleasant apparitions in their house, during the night, and that they thought somebody from their own sect was placing curses on them. The leaders of their temple had been to the house, to exorcise it, but the problems still continued. This house was not in the prayer-walk triangle but was close by and the woman, whom they felt had placed curses on them, did live in the triangle. I went to visit their house, with Salim and Shamim, who understood their culture better, and we prayed for it from top to bottom, in every room, cleansing it with holy water. We continued to pray for that couple for about a year and then they moved to another part of the city.

Another day two women, who also lived in the triangle, came to the church, to complain about Jericho's plans for a training centre. Once they had heard the real vision (rather than the lies being circulated), they were fine about it and wanted to support its development. During the course of the conversation, one of the women (whom we later learnt had been involved in prostitution when she was younger) told me about some health problems she had. She was willing to accept prayer for these and I visited her house with Janet to pray for her. These prayer sessions continued for a while and her health did improve, as the pain in a frozen shoulder was eased. She then told us that she often saw a ghostly woman standing in her house and wondered whether we could deal with it for her. Whilst we were there, Janet saw this apparition herself, and perceived that it was harmless. However, she did encourage the spirit to go to her rest and to leave the house alone in future. It was never seen again there. Not long after, this women and her neighbour left the triangle and moved to other parts of the city.

All these incidents helped us to see why there had been such a problem in getting a Christian project off the ground; the whole area had been in the grip of occult influences for many years and it is possible that the prayer walks and the house cleansings had the effect of lessening their power over Balsall Heath. By 1995, we had become aware of certain territorial spirits, which were associated with the problems of the area: drugs, gambling, prostitution, witchcraft, violence, lies and deception. Janet prayed daily for the area and for the Jericho Project and, one day during her prayers she received the word 'Apollyon'. She found reference to this in Revelations:

> "They had as king over them the angel of the Abyss, whose name in Hebrew is Abaddon, and in Greek, Apollyon."
> Rev. 9:11 (NIV)

From this we concluded that there was an overriding spirit in Balsall Heath controlling all of the darker activities there, the spirit of Apollyon. The abyss is the sump of mankind – the place where all the dirt and evil collects and that sometimes this overflows onto the surface. This triangle where we conducted our prayer walk could have been the abyss of Birmingham. We would like to think that persistent prayer helped to win the battle over Balsall Heath, which was at that time the sump of the city.

During the early days of the Jericho Project, a partnership had formed with another local, black-led church, the Church of God of Prophecy. People from this church joined with the prayer group to pray for the area and they also shared their own vision for the community development of their own church. The Jericho Project, through Jane Gallagher, was able to help them to find the funds to have their church modified to open a centre for people from the African Caribbean community who were in need, especially those at risk of a mental health problem. They named this, The Good Neighbour Centre, and appointed a psychiatric nurse, Trevor Minto, to be the manager of this centre. The Good Neighbour Centre eventually grew to the point where it was able to become a charity in its own right and to become independent of Jericho. Trevor later left and was replaced at the centre by Penny Howe, who had been one of the founder members of the early morning prayer group.

Over all of this period there had been regular meetings taking place of local residents' associations. They met with the police and with the local authority because they were so angry about prostitution and all the other crime associated with it. These were tough times for the police! Then a self-styled local community leader started working closely with the Muslim men in the area. He encouraged them not to wait for the police to act any longer but to take their own vigilante action. Large groups of them started sitting on street corners to deter prostitution; they took the registration numbers of cars involved in kerb crawling and passed them on to the police. If this had been all that they did, it would have been OK, but many of the vigilantes (who called themselves pickets!) became abusive towards the women and any visitors they might have, spitting at them and throwing stones. They even set up a large catapult, to launch rocks at the (double-glazed) house window of one of the women who resisted moving from the area; they also tried to put petrol bombs through her letterbox, until she sealed it up. This kind of abusive behaviour was also directed towards a team of nuns who worked gently among the women in prostitution. Several people openly opposed this approach in a community meeting and became greatly disliked by the community leader and the leader of the pickets and his henchmen.

C became very angry about what was happening and was seen on TV news, shouting at the pickets. She wanted it to be known that several of the men on the picket lines were pimps or punters themselves and were behaving hypocritically by their action. Others also explained to the media that the men on the picket lines were happy to take the money made from immoral earnings in their local shops and the taxi-drivers from the same community were happy to receive large tips from clients who asked them to wait for them. "And now they are protesting about how immoral we are," she stated. "Who do you think the girls were renting rooms from?" Despite all this, C soon realised that there was no use in resisting the actions of the pickets, as they had gained the support of the police and national government. She, too, moved away from the triangle of streets and we almost lost touch with her. I was later to visit her to find that one of her sons was in prison for drug-related criminal activity. This might have been averted, if the family had not been driven out of the area, thus losing the support that they had been receiving.

THIS DARK PHOTOGRAPH APPEARED IN "THE GUARDIAN" ON JULY 23RD 1994, SHOWING PICKETS ABUSING ONE OF THE WOMEN

One day, whilst I was working in my office at the church, E (who was involved in prostitution and who lived with her three children in the triangle of streets) sent her daughter across, to ask for help. They were trapped in their home, with gangs of Arab youths throwing stones at the windows. Her daughter had escaped out of the back door and had rushed across the road for sanctuary in the church. E and her family had to be re-housed a mile away but the pickets followed her there and she had to be re-housed a second time.

THIS PHOTOGRAPH OF MEN ON A PICKET LINE APPEARED IN "THE TIMES" ON JULY 21ST 1994, ALONGSIDE THE HEADLINE "PAVEMENT PICKETS BANISH PROSTITUTION"

Several of the women, whom the nuns and the Jericho Project were working with, had been close to leaving prostitution, or escaping from their pimp, but the vigilante action put paid to all of that. A horrifying consequence of this was that the pimps moved the younger girls out of the area and kept them locked in flats, where they could bring clients to them – this was a form of kidnapping! The remainder of the women moved into saunas or to another part of the city. Prostitution had not been eradicated from Birmingham but merely shifted to other areas, yet the pickets, and their leader, claimed success and were heralded nationally for a good piece of community action. Copycat activities began to spring up in other cities. And it is worrying that the present policy of appointing neighbourhood wardens in certain areas had its roots in local actions like this one. It is a pity that Government has not seen that it is unwise to do this in areas religious division – have they not learned from Northern Ireland – or even Iraq?

There is no doubt that Balsall Heath changed for the better, as a result of the vigilante action - but at what cost? It resulted in a divided community, people becoming homeless and some of the Asian youths being arrested for violent activity. One of them I knew well, for he had been attending the drop-in, looking for a job. After a two-year prison sentence for his violent behaviour, it became much harder for him to find employment. I do not believe that two wrongs make a right and will therefore always oppose this type of action. However, Balsall Heath could no longer be construed as the sump of the city. Was this because of our prayer walk, or because of vigilante action?

The Jericho Project had become formally constituted as a registered charity and a charitable company in 1993 and, throughout this period, we continued to try to get the training centre project off the ground. Because of opposition at the planning stage, it was decided to ditch plans for a café but to continue with the rest of the vision. As a result, city council approval was given to go ahead with a package of funding from the housing association and the inner city partnership programme. The building work for the new centre went out to tender and a builder was selected. Then, three days before the builders were due to start on site, the City Council suddenly withdrew their funding support. The training project went into reversal for a second time. This happened in 1994.

The Management Committee decided that the Jericho Project had been wronged by the City Council, as it had been led to believe that funding would be forthcoming and had committed it's own funds into the project. On a recommendation by the local MP (Rt. Hon. Roy Hattersley), the committee put in a complaint to the local authority ombudsman. After some deliberation, the ombudsman ruled that the Jericho Project did not have a case. It was another low period for the project.

Jane Gallagher, who had been helping to develop the project and to link with statutory authorities, had to leave for another job, as the money to pay her ran out. We might have been tempted to give up on the vision, especially as funding for me to work in the community was also running out. I didn't look for another job because I felt strongly that the Lord wanted me to continue to work in Balsall Heath – that, indeed, this was to be a test of my faith. Jane helped to find some short-term European funding, which enabled me to do some research into how other European countries were dealing with prostitution issues, especially in finding exit strategies to enable the women to leave prostitution. I travelled to Paris with a colleague, Maud, to study some excellent projects there, run under the umbrella of an organisation (funded by the French national government) called "L'Amicale du Nid". There were drop-in facilities for the women, to discuss their options, outreach teams, safe houses, emergency overnight accommodation, counselling support, help with obtaining housing and legal help with prosecuting pimps. One project that struck a strong chord was called "Atelier Dagobert". This project, just outside Paris, offered work experience on a factory production line, together with basic skills training and help in getting a permanent job, to women who wished to leave prostitution. The project had an 80% success rate in helping the women into normal employment at the end of their placement. Most of them went into care work.

Part of this research had also involved carrying out interviews with the women (and girls) involved in prostitution in Birmingham. Fortunately, this was begun before the vigilante action had cleared the streets of prostitutes but, because of the action, it was only possible to include a small sample; the research involved talking to women on street corners and in windows. From this research, it was learnt that almost three quarters of the women had started in prostitution before they were 19 years old and 80% of them had experienced severe childhood trauma. Some of the stories they told were horrific and included violent alcoholic fathers, being locked in a cellar, sexual abuse, rejecting step parents, running away from home at an early age and living in a graveyard. One third of the cohort had been brought up in care. Only a quarter of the women interviewed had stayed at school long enough to take any qualifications; one had never been to school, two had been expelled, another had gone to a mother and baby home when she was 14, another had left school at 12, when she ran away from home. As a result, most of the women interviewed were semi-literate and their options for normal employment were therefore very limited. All of the women expressed an interest in attending a training course and half said they would like to leave prostitution. Half the group admitted to being on drugs at some time and one third had a criminal record (usually for soliciting).

The results of the research were written up in a booklet entitled, "A Study of the Networks of Support Available to Women who wish to Leave Prostitution". It was given to everybody attending an inter-agency conference, called in Birmingham to disseminate the results of the research, in the hope that some of the ideas from France, Belgium and elsewhere might be taken on in this country. Interestingly, both the police and the probation service wanted to take some action and a working group was set up, to look at the issue of under-age prostitution. As a result, a pilot study began in Wolverhampton, in which there was a partnership between police and social services to deal with the under-age girls as victims of sexual abuse rather than criminals. This was a huge breakthrough but, sadly, there was little enthusiasm for implementing some of the French ideas in this country and such networks still do not exist in the city. Because of the action of the vigilantes in Balsall Heath, it was impossible for the Jericho Project to try to pioneer such networks also. The whole issue of prostitution was too much of a hot potato for the area.

The booklet was also sent to local politicians (councillors and MPs) with little response, apart from the following, rather negative and cynical, reply from a (Conservative) MP:

"*I certainly think it is very commendable that women who are prostitutes should be given an opportunity to get out of the trade. It would only peripherally affect the situation in Birmingham, I fear. I am pretty sure that the overwhelming majority of women plying this unpleasant trade on our streets are doing it because they want to do it and it is fairly easy money. I just don't believe we could clear the problem up by persuading them all not to be prostitutes any more – much as I would like to find such a good solution.*"

The fact that half of the women interviewed wanted to leave prostitution (and all of them were interested in some form of training) seemed to have passed her by.

By the time this research had finished, only a few months funding remained in Jericho's bank account to cover my salary and the Management Committee were concerned about their responsibility as my employer. They felt they should consider redundancy for when the money did run out, so that they complied properly with employment law. The Chairman, Pastor John, wrote me a letter, as follows:

"*I am sorry to inform you that, as from the first day of August, you will be laid off from work for a period of one month, or until such time as sufficient funds are available to be able to pay you. The situation will be reviewed during the last week of August. Should the situation remain the same after two months, we may face a redundancy situation.*

I am deeply sorry about this and trust that funding will soon be given."

Fortunately, the committee did not need to take the action of making me redundant. What happened was another astonishing example of God's provision. There was one month in which I was not paid but I carried on working anyway. During that month, out of the blue, three separate

Christian friends, who did not know each other and who did not know the situation within Jericho, wrote to me saying that they felt the Lord wanted them to send me some money. Their cheques totalled the amount I would have received that month in my salary cheque! Another example of God's golden notes falling on those doing his work! He is marvellous in the way he provides for us! My faith was strengthened by this provision and, within a month, further European and UK charitable funds were made available to enable me to continue to work in the local community.

The land in the triangle, where it was planned to build the training centre, was also lost during this period. The housing association, which had bought the land in order to work in partnership with the Jericho Project, decided that they could not wait for us to get another funding package together. They built some family homes on the land. The project was in reversal for a third time!

During all of this period, the drop-in facility in the church hall had continued to run, to enable unemployed people to look for work. Some statistics were prepared about all the unemployed people who had attended the drop-in, to identify which of them had been the most successful in obtaining work. The data showed that certain people were less likely to get jobs than others, mainly because employers did not want them. These included:

- The very long-term unemployed (5+ years)
- People with no qualifications
- Ex-offenders
- People who could not speak or write English
- People who were disabled
- The homeless
- People who had had a drug or alcohol addiction.

The management committee of Jericho was challenged by this data. They knew that Jesus came to help especially those people whom nobody else wants. In this modern context, it was clear that the above groups were those that employers did not want, and therefore the Jericho Project should demonstrate a loving attitude towards them by showing that it wanted them. It was suggested that Jericho should become an employer itself and should offer jobs to these very people. But how could it do this? The site in the triangle had been lost, the money had been withdrawn and the local community seemed utterly opposed to the Jericho Project (we later learnt that one reason for the opposition – and the City Council's withdrawal of funds - was that an Islamic group had wanted to set up their own training centre and the City Council had refused them funding for it; the City Council did not feel it expedient to then fund a Christian project).

In 1995-96, we heard about a model, pioneered in Scotland – the ILM model (intermediate labour market). In this model, which had some things in common with the Atelier Dagobert project for ex-prostitutes in Paris, which had so impressed me, unemployed people were offered temporary paid work, with training and personal development, to prepare them for a real job. People attending such schemes had a much higher success rate in obtaining work than those attending other (more training based) schemes.

It was decided to seek funding to try out this model in Balsall Heath. Initially, it was planned to pilot it, by renting out some small industrial premises in the area. Then, a large warehouse, with a shop unit at the front, came onto the market. It was not far from the church, was three times larger than the building that had been planned for the triangle site and would cost less. Jericho's management committee decided to try and get the money together to buy the warehouse and to set up an ILM project there. The total cost would be about £400,000 to buy and refurbish the warehouse appropriately and funds to pay a staff team would be additional to that. It would be another step of faith!

About that time, a pensioner from my own church, Millie, came up to me and said,

"I feel the Lord wants me to give some money to the Jericho Project," and she thrust a £5 note into my hand. For a pensioner at that time, £5 was a lot of money – like a widow's mite – and this was recognised this as a powerful and sacrificial gift.

> *"As he looked up, Jesus saw the rich putting their gifts into the temple treasury.*
> *He also saw a poor widow put in two very small copper coins. "I tell you the truth," he said, "this poor widow has put in more than all the others. All these people gave their gifts out of their wealth; but she out of her poverty put in all she had to live on.""*
> Luke 21: 1-4 (NIV)

Millie's gift was taken to Jericho's Wednesday prayer group, who prayed over it, thanked God for it and asked him to multiply it according to the needs of the project. In fact, the group asked God to multiply it 100,000 times, to enable us to buy this warehouse and to start a project there! And the Wednesday prayer group continued that practice every time a cheque or donation was received for the work and it still continues to do that. Ever since then, God has supplied for all the financial needs of the Jericho Project.

An application was made for European Regional Development Fund monies, as well as to other UK statutory sources of funds (English Partnerships) and charitable trusts for the 50% match needed, and eventually decisions were made in favour of the ILM project. Another pensioner (a former pastor of mine, now a widower and well into his eighties) felt he wanted to help launch the project and generously donated the value of his Halifax windfall shares. This was a widower's mite! Another powerful and sacrificial gift. Other charitable trusts also gave grants, as did the Church Urban Fund; all of these grants and donations together came to the amount that was needed to buy the warehouse and make minor refurbishments.

Then, another application was made to the European Social Fund (Employment-Integra) to pay for a staff team and running costs, as well as wages for the long-term unemployed staff that would come onto the project. This would cover the revenue costs for the first 18 months.

The grants all came through in the autumn of 1998, eleven years after John Mallard had first shared his vision with me. God had answered the prayer request of multiplying the £5 note by 100,000! Indeed, he had given us more than that. He had provided for the project to begin. Eileen's vision of golden notes showering down on Gilgal had also become true for Jericho!

But, I believe that our experiences over these 11 years have shown that the Lord requires perseverance from us as well, if his purposes are to be fulfilled in difficult areas (especially in the sump of the city). To write the story of how the money came together does not give justice to all the pain (and almost despair) that was present during the last few months, as decisions were awaited from the various funding bodies. There were times during those few months when it seemed as if one tranche of money would come through and not another and then it would seem as if all of it had been lost. I can remember a period when I thought we might be able to buy the warehouse but not have enough money for a staff team – this led to visions of me sitting in this huge warehouse on my own, trying to get the new project off the ground alone! Fortunately, this was one vision that never came to fulfilment. At times, I also felt unsupported in the huge task that was ahead, with a total lack of enthusiasm for the vision from potential partners and colleagues. This got me down so much during the summer of 1998, that I felt like giving up altogether. I can remember spending hours on my knees in prayer saying,

"Lord, are you sure you want me to spend all my time and my energy on this? What about the destiny I thought you had placed on my life? And what about the people in the community of Balsall Heath who need my help? Shouldn't I be spending time with them instead of all this bureaucracy?"

And his answer came to me as clear as a bell,

"This is your destiny!"

Despite these reassurances, there was one period in August 1998, when I was so worn out and despairing about the whole thing and I went to a Sunday morning service in my own church in this frame of mind. That day we had a visiting preacher, Rev. Kate Coleman from London. She preached on the theme of perseverance and, at the end of the service, invited people in need to go forward for prayer. I walked forward with tears streaming down my face. Kate prayed for me and I felt renewed and restored. The Lord had clearly sent Kate at my time of need, to give me the strength to keep going. Within a month of this, all the money had come through and the Jericho Project was able to buy the warehouse and appoint a team of people to run the ILM project.

The first staff team included five people, two of whom had been helping as volunteers. One of them, Shamim, had been a member of the Wednesday prayer team and the prayer walk; she was to become responsible for the retail outlet of the warehouse. Another of them, Maia, a former Macedonian refugee and a Christian, had originally come to the project for help to find work. She started as Project Administrator. The first manager of the project was Kees Blom, whose wife, Maria, had received the original three-part prophecy. He was to be followed in the role later by John Mallard's son, Roger. Other staff included Edith Maynard, who had applied to work for the project because she felt that God had called her to this, and Joanne Green. Shamim's husband, Salim was also to join the project at a later stage, by offering maths tuition to the trainee placements but, before that happened, Shamim's salary from Jericho was to enable her husband to continue an inner city evangelical ministry among the Asian communities in the city. The first staff team was multi-racial, which was most appropriate for the community that was being served.

**THE WAREHOUSE BUILDING WITH SHOP UNIT AT
THE FRONT**

SOME EARLY MEMBERS OF THE STAFF TEAM:
Jacki, Joanne, Sylvia, Maia, Roger, Shamim and Edith

When we first moved into the warehouse in December 1998, it was much too large for our needs – we were rattling around in there - but now, five years on, the work has increased so much, that it is too small. It is three times bigger than the training centre that would have been built on the empty site in the triangle opposite the church – the Lord really knew what he was doing in focusing attention on a bigger place.

Some of the people who were in most difficulties in the local community came onto the project as beneficiary staff in the first few months. At least three of the female beneficiaries had been in prostitution before and several had previously had drugs' problems; several were ex-offenders and had spent time in the local prison (the prison over which hangs a heavy spirit of grief).

When the pickets (who were still operating in the area) got wind of the fact that Jericho now owned the warehouse and were employing ex-prostitutes, they tried to get the project closed. All kinds of false rumours were circulated about the Jericho Project again; one rumour was that it was misappropriating city council funds. Since Jericho was receiving no city council funds at that time, this rumour was easily scotched. However, when the first tranche of revenue funding ran out eighteen months' later, an application had to be made for local funds to continue the project and the application went before a local committee for approval. The leader of the pickets was a member of this committee and he brought several of his group along to the meeting to try and block Jericho's application. A decision about funding for Jericho was therefore postponed (because of the size of the opposing group), whilst the chairman sought further information. Opposition to Jericho's work in the area was continuing! It was another time of reversal. Despite all the good beginnings of the ILM project, with people already moving into real jobs, it looked as if the project would have to end.

During this period, I felt again that the Lord was urging me to go into a lion's den (as he had several years earlier, when I went to visit the Wiccan). This time God wanted me to go alone to visit the leader of the pickets in his home. As this man had a daytime job, an evening appointment had to be made and, when I arrived at his home, he was waiting for me with several of his group of supporters. I felt quite threatened by this but spoke to him as gently and pleasantly as I could, taking the opportunity to explain to him that we were not encouraging prostitution but helping the women to get out of it. It appeared that one woman in particular was concerning him who was on the Jericho ILM project at that time. They felt frustrated with her, as they had not been able to drive her out of her house (he did not mention the giant catapult that had been used to launch bricks against her windows). I was able to tell them that she had already gained a training qualification whilst with the Jericho Project, which should help her to get alternative employment. By the end of the meeting, I did not think I had been able to change their minds about the Jericho Project, but the Lord was clearly at work. This group never openly opposed the project again and the application for local funds was eventually approved. I believe that, in both of these visits to "lion's dens", the Lord was using the principle of strength in weakness, expounded by St. Paul in his letters:

> *"My gracious power is all you need. My power works best in your weakness."*
> 2 Corinthians 12:9 (NLT).

The project was able to continue for another six months, to bridge the gap until more substantial European funding became available again.

In a similar way, the Lord had used another of his coincidences, when I found myself attending a meeting at which the City Council officer was present – the one who had blocked the original Inner City Partnership bid for funds to build the training centre in the triangle. In a lull during discussions, when others had left for refreshments, the Lord made it clear to me that I was to tell him that we, in the Jericho Project, bore him no grudge for what had happened in the past. And, in a miraculous turn of events, seven years after that withdrawal of funding, the City Council agreed to cover all the revenue costs of the project. The Lord certainly does work in mysterious ways.

A community business was set up to run the employment project (ILM), which then sub-contracted for the Government's New Deal funding for unemployed people, to help run the project. Kees Blom managed the business for about a year and was then replaced by John's son, Roger, who expanded the staff team and built up the shop over the next three years. The present manager is my son, Ben, who started a year and a half ago. He now leads a staff team of 12. The community business runs a multi-purpose shop and has a manufacturing arm, of printing and embroidering T-shirts and other garments and goods. A recent development has been the addition of a jobsearch unit, which helps other New Deal projects to get their beneficiaries into work.

From the start it was decided that special efforts had to be made to ensure that the ILM project was there for the most disadvantaged people and so criteria were introduced to make sure this happened. People coming to work as beneficiaries of the project needed to be at least two years unemployed to qualify and also to have another labour market disadvantage. They are then offered a package of three days paid work, one day training (working towards an NVQ qualification) and one day of personal development, which includes basic skills training (literacy, numeracy and/or English as a Second Language), jobsearch training, driving theory lessons and other social support (as needed – several come with debt problems, homelessness or court cases hanging over them). Work placements are available in the shop (retail), as print assistants (T-shirts), in graphic design, office administration, catering (there is a sandwich bar in the shop), warehouse assistant, maintenance and marketing.

When the project first started, there was only one computer for the work but now the community business has expanded so much that it owns several specialist computers for graphic design work, as well as a bank of new computers for the job search programme, where beneficiary staff can learn to search the internet for employment opportunities.

Jericho Community Business has now become one of the best voluntary sector New Deal projects in the city of Birmingham, as it has a high success rate in getting people onto further employment at the end of their placement; it is also the only New Deal project run by the voluntary sector, which values their unemployed cohort by paying them a wage.

Since Jericho first started taking unemployed people onto its staff in January 1999, hundreds of people have been helped by it (about 100 per year), most of them young people from ethnic minority groups, aged under 25 years, with three quarters of them being male. Ironically (since local Muslims had opposed the project so much in the early stages), about 60% of people helped by the project are of the Muslim faith. It is an opportunity to show Christian love in action. One previous Muslim employee has made the following remark about us:

"When I first came onto the project, I wanted to make trouble for you Christians, but I was shown so much respect that I changed my mind."

Another said,

"You Christians are different. I am impressed because you are all so honest!"

Most people coming onto the project, as well as being long-term unemployed, have had other disadvantages in their lives, such as no educational qualifications (30%), being an ex-offender (15%), having chronic illness (10%), being disabled (10%), homeless (5%) or in debt (5%). Lone parents, ex-addicts, prostitutes and refugees have also been helped with short-term, transitional employment, to prepare them for a real job.

More than half have gone onto further employment; the majority gained basic skills qualifications (in many cases, the first academic achievement they had ever attained) and all achieved an NVQ qualification in their chosen area of work; some went onto further training.

The following text boxes give the stories (in their own words) of two people who were helped by the project; one had a disability (Asperger syndrome) and the other was very long-term unemployed.

J's STORY

I left school when I was 16 and then went to Bournville College for 4 years where I did various courses involving office skills and gained an NVQ level 1 in administration.

When I left college I had difficulty finding a job because I have Asperger Syndrome, an autistic spectrum disorder. Eventually, my Disability Employment Advisor arranged for me to come to Jericho for 6 weeks work preparation. After that I worked voluntarily at Jericho and was eventually offered a 12-month contract. When that expired I continued as a volunteer, whilst being helped with my job search by the Aspire employment service who are dedicated to helping people with my disability. I eventually was offered a short-term contract within the NHS, which has now been extended to March 2005.

My time at Jericho gave me valuable experience in using, maintaining and updating my office skills. It helped me gain confidence in my own ability and helped me to learn how to work with other people, which I found difficult. As a result, Jericho gave me a good reference when I applied for jobs.

I am very grateful for the help given me by Jericho and am sure that my time there helped me in being successful in gaining a job.

E's STORY

I was unemployed for 9 years during the 1990's and had tried all kinds of ways to get a job; including attending various kinds of training (electronics, music technology, computer maintenance, IT skills) but none of this did any good. In 2002, I was referred to the Jericho Community Business for a six-month placement in administration. I was hoping that this would update my skills for the current jobs' market. Whilst at Jericho, I had opportunities to do some minor accounting work and to prepare documents, reports and letters. I had practice in using Microsoft Word and Access on the computer.

I believe that I developed a professional telephone manner as a result of undertaking reception and switchboard duties at Jericho and I also learnt how to maintain manual filing systems and general tasks, such as photocopying and faxing.

During my time at Jericho, I was referred for an interview with Capita Business Services Ltd., a partner organisation working with Jericho. During the interview, I had to make a presentation and received help in preparing for this from the Jericho jobsearch unit. I was successful in this interview and have kept my job as an Administrator within Capita for a year and a half now. In this job, I have extended my experience in accounting work, database maintenance and reception work and have had opportunities in the training and management of temporary staff there.

Jericho Community Business helped me to make a new start in my life.

Several of the people coming onto the Jericho ILM project had spent time in Birmingham prison (Winson Green). Whilst Jericho cannot claim to have instantly turned their lives around, these people have taken their first faltering steps towards a life that is crime-free. One of Jericho's roles has been to act as an advocate in the courts, where magistrates and judges seem relieved to find that there is an alternative to further incarceration.

The following photographs give some idea of what the Jericho Community Business (ILM) is doing at present.

WORKING IN THE WAREHOUSE

PLACEMENTS ARE AVAILABLE IN GRAPHIC AND WEB DESIGN

**JERICHO NOW OWNS AN EMBRIODERY MACHINE AND
OFFERS PLACEMENTS IN THIS TYPE OF WORK**

BENEFICIARY STAFF IN THE COMMUNITY SHOP

SOME OF THE CURRENT STAFF AND BENEFICIARIES OUTSIDE THE SHOP

In November 2002, a new section of the work began: a women-only project, which offers part-time, paid work to women returnees. This project mainly takes on women from the Asian community, many of whom have never worked and never attended a training class before. They have an opportunity to attend classes in English and their placement is in sewing machining. It is managed by one of Jericho's previous long-term unemployed beneficiaries. As a result of this project, the community business has been able to expand to offer a service of garments, curtains and other items made to order and is even now planning to extend the business to include a washing and ironing service. This aspect of the business is doing extremely well. Some of the women have already found employment elsewhere. The following photograph shows two of the women on the project.

TWO OF THE WOMEN ON THE NEW WOMEN'S SEWING MACHINING -PROJECT

Now, Jericho is about to start another new arm of its work amongst the unemployed. This latest initiative is to be a training project in construction skills, particularly targeting people who have had a drugs' problem or who have been homeless, with a minor mental health problem. This project, Renaissance-21, is due to start in 2004. Beneficiaries on this project will receive their work experience on-site in the repair of council houses, which will eventually be adapted to provide community housing, with live-in support, for this client group. This project has already been through one reversal but we do believe that, through it, God will provide a team of skilled building workers who may help with the refurbishment of other derelict premises in the city.

"Your people will rebuild the ancient ruins and will raise up the ancient foundations; you will be called Repairer of Broken Walls, Restorer of Streets with Dwellings."
Isaiah 58: 12 (NIV)

The project has come so far since John Mallard first shared his God-given vision with me in 1987. Neither of us could have believed at that time how much God would do through the vision (nor how long it would take to get it off the ground). Since those early beginnings, there has been the Good Neighbour Centre, set up in the nearby Church of God of Prophecy, the expansion of the drop-in centre in the church hall to include jobsearch and other social support, the opening of the Jericho Community Business, offering ILM placements for the long-term unemployed in the large warehouse (now owned by Jericho), the starting of an ILM project for women returnees and (just about to begin) the Renaissance-21 Project, to provide training with personal development support in construction skills for ex-drug users and other people who have been homeless, with minor mental health problems.

John has now retired and Darrell has taken his place as chairman of Jericho. But, I am so pleased that John saw the fulfilment of the vision that God had given him before his retirement.

Not long ago, an ecumenical group of Christians in Balsall Heath met to pray for the area. They were standing on the pavement opposite the Jericho warehouse. During the prayers, one of the group, Marion, looked up and saw a rainbow in the sky, spanning right across the top of the Jericho building. She believed this to be deeply significant and shared it with me, not knowing about the rainbow vision that had previously been given to Bill Dixon several years earlier, when he received a promise from God:

"All that I have promised I will do, I will do!"

I believe that this sign, given to Marion, reinforces the promise given to Bill and provides another link between the two projects.

When God speaks, his will prevails but, as shown by the Jericho Community Project, it is usually not without a struggle, because the forces of evil always try to oppose his will. The Jericho Project is a very good example of how the battle between darkness and light was eventually won by God.

> *"Shine out among them like beacon lights, holding out to them the Word of Life."*
> Philippians 2: 15-16 (LB)

It has been a long and exciting journey, which is still not over, for there are still those who do not want the project to succeed. It was a much longer struggle to get Jericho off the ground than it was for Gilgal (11 years compared to 8 years) but both projects demonstrate that, when God speaks, perseverance is needed, if his vision is to be seen through to completion. Like Gilgal, Jericho has also had a huge impact on the city, as it is the largest ILM (intermediate labour market) project in the city offering hope to the long-term unemployed. We believe it to be a powerful example of God's vision and his provision for his will to be fulfilled.

JERICHO

breaking down the barriers

CHAPTER FOUR

Bethel!

"How precious is your constant love, O Lord!
All humanity takes refuge in the shadow of your wings.
You feed them with blessings from your own table
And let them drink from your rivers of delight."
Psalm 36: 7-8 (LB)

The vision for Bethel came much later – in March 2001 - well after the Jericho Community Business had been established - it had now been running smoothly for three years and Gilgal was already seven years old by this time. I had been through a barren period in terms of my prayer life, as I had not heard God speaking to me for some time. The early days of Jericho had drained me and I was tired and had been in poor health. God knew this and had, perhaps, given some breathing space before speaking again, with a further revelation of his will for the city, within the three-part prophecy.

The revelation happened this way. I was praying with some friends in a house group; they had been studying the Bible and meditating on what was meant in Matt. 3:16 (the baptism of Jesus), especially by the words "the heavens were opened to him". Following the Bible study, there was a time of worship and prayer - a time of waiting on God. As I rested in God's presence, I saw a picture of Jesus at his baptism – it was an awe-inspiring picture. The place was filled with a brilliant light and angels were ascending and descending within that light. A dove was there, the Holy Spirit, mingling with the angels. The picture took my breath away.

I was deeply affected by this vision and continued to seek its meaning over a period of days. I was aware that, in the Bible, God frequently accompanied a commissioning or revelation to his people with a vision of his glory (Gen. 28;

Exod.3 and 33: 18-22; Isaiah 6; Ezek. 1; Dan. 10; Acts 9; Rev. 1: 9-18). I also remembered the prayer meeting at the beginning of Jericho, when John Mallard and I had been praying for confirmation of that vision and had seen a brilliant fulgent light, lighting up the whole Balsall Heath area.

I spent the next few days in fasting and prayer, seeking the meaning of this new vision. During my prayers, God reminded me of its similarity with the dream given to Jacob at Bethel, when he saw angels ascending and descending on a ladder up to heaven.

> *"(Jacob) had a dream in which he saw a stairway resting on the earth with its top reaching to heaven, and the angels of God were ascending and descending on it. There above it stood the Lord."*
> Genesis 28: 12-13 (NIV)

Jacob believed that he had seen the gate of heaven and he named the place where he had this dream, Bethel (Genesis 28: 10-19). I turned to this passage in the Bible and, as I read it, something suddenly clicked with me: the name Jacob had given to the place where he had his dream, Bethel, was the same name that Maria had been given as the third part of God's revelation for the city. Then, within me, I heard these words:

"The time is now right for the third part of Maria's prophecy to take place - Bethel. It is to be a Christian Healing Centre and a Healthy Living Centre."

Wow! I was bowled over by this! Was God speaking again, after all these months of dryness?

I shared the revelation with my house group the following week and, over the next few weeks they prayed about it. Gradually, through them, God also gave confirmation, by images and Bible passages of cleansing water, fountains, streams and healing leaves (Ezek. 47: 1-12; Rev. 22: 1-2; Psalm 36: 7-9; Psalm 51: 7; Psalm 18: 4-19). Somebody also received a picture of people trapped in mud, who needed to be drawn out of it and cleansed with water from a fresh sparkling stream.

I felt drawn to share the vision with Wai Lan Liu, also from my church, who became very excited because the Lord had been speaking to her in a similar way and urging her to share with me, though for her, the healing ministry was to be purely for drug and alcohol addicts. Wai Lan and I had travelled together to Hong Kong seven years earlier, to visit the work carried out amongst heroin addicts there by Jackie Pullinger and her team and Wai Lan now felt that the Lord was wanting her to set up a healing ministry for addicts in this country, similar to the Hong Kong work. We decided to call together a meeting of all the people in the city whom we knew were involved in a healing or prayer counselling ministry or with drug addicts, and we shared with them what God was saying to us. It was good to meet with other Christians who felt called to similar ministries; they came from all different denominations of the Church, as well as from house churches.

The group continued to meet monthly to pray together and eventually became known as the Bethel Network. A directory was produced and circulated, which listed all the Christian agencies involved in prayer, counselling, healing or rehabilitation ministries within Greater Birmingham.

During prayer in this group, a number of words of knowledge were given, as well as pictures, each confirming the vision that the Lord had given me. In particular, there were images of people trapped in mud, who were being drawn out and cleansed with clear water – the same images that had been given to a different person in the house group. It was also felt that, when this healing centre opened, it would act as a resource for all the churches in the city. Indeed, it would act to unite them.

I asked the Lord what characteristics the healing centre should have and he showed me a picture of an entrance to a building, with some glass doors and a reception desk. I felt he was saying that the centre should offer the following:

- Healing services, where people can receive prayer with the laying on of hands;
- A welcoming place where people can walk in off the streets to receive healing prayer and/or counselling;
- A place where prayer ministry and/or counselling would take place by appointment;
- A place where training in healing ministry and prayer counselling would take place;
- Emergency overnight accommodation for people in desperate need, who came in off the streets;
- Live-in accommodation for manager/s or night staff;
- Activities that would promote healthy living.

Thus, out of the Bethel vision would come a two-pronged focus: activities offering a Christian ministry of healing and prayer; and activities associated with the promotion of healthy living, some of which might be of a campaigning nature.

As this group continued to meet together, I learnt that five of them had also felt that God was calling them to open a special centre (Wai Lan, Pat, Graham, Martin and Ian), though the vision for each of their centres was a little different from the vision God had given me. Also, we learnt that another Centre for Health & Healing was already being developed at the historic St. Martin's Church in the Bullring; Mike Murkin, the new director of this, was a former colleague of mine, who had previously served on the Management Committee of the Jericho Project. Each of the six visions was slightly different, with emphases on different client groups and styles of ministry.

Then, somebody received a picture of a flower and another felt that the meaning of this was that each of the new centres would be like petals and that one main centre would service them all and bring unity to the whole. The word "unity" was given as a word of knowledge.

The group continued to meet to pray together but then a time of confusion began, which I believe to be the time of Bethel's first reversal.

Wai Lan decided to split off and to concentrate on her own training (with Ellel Ministries) and in developing a residential centre for drug addicts. Martin also felt that the vision God had given him was to for him to develop alone, in conjunction with the church that he pastored – it was also to provide a range of social support services, as well as a healing ministry. Graham, who had previously managed a Christian counselling centre in another part of the city, The Vine, which had closed four years earlier, felt that the Lord was telling him the time was not yet right. Ian was severely injured in a road accident. Pat and her husband became ill but both she and Mike kept in touch. Now, over a year later, the Centre for Health and Healing at St. Martin's in the Bullring has opened. And I believe it to be another miracle of God's purposes being fulfilled in the city. Amazingly, the city planners, in developing the new Bullring, incorporated the church as a part of a new shopping complex, opening onto a square – named St. Martin's Square. The shopping complex has been so busy and people have been flocking into the church and the healing centre from the square. Their weekly healing services are attended by up to 150 people and their counselling team have full diaries of appointments. So God has already brought about the vision of the team at St. Martin's but I believe that the vision he gave me for a healing centre was for another place, with different facilities on offer from those at St. Martin's.

Some months ago, I put together a Business Plan, describing the vision for a healing centre/ healthy living centre and costed it out; this was sent to key people in the secular health networks, in the hope that it would generate funds to set up a healing centre. By now, I had a great deal of practice in writing business plans and raising funds, but this one had no impact at all. These people treated me as if I were a bit crazy – a bumbling, amateurish, Christian do-gooder, who had little knowledge of the professional health field (which was far from the truth). None showed any interest in funding or facilitating such a centre. We could have applied for funding from the New Opportunities Fund (which is earmarked for local healthy living centres) but this was lottery funding and required local communities to work together to develop such a centre. After the experience of setting up Jericho, I could not see local Muslim groups agreeing to a healing centre where people were prayed for in the name of Jesus. As with Gilgal and Jericho before, I became discouraged.

However, in the meantime, Wai Lan and I had shared our visions jointly with our own church and had received encouragement from them. As they were carrying the whole weight of the Gilgal vision, I had not felt that I should expect them to also take on Bethel. However, not long after, the Lord gave our church something of a challenge, through studying the book of Haggai.

> *"Give careful thought to your ways. You have planted much, but have harvested little. You eat, but never have enough. You drink but never have your fill. You put on clothes but are not warm. You earn wages, only to put them in a purse with holes in it."*
> Haggai 1: 5-6 (NIV)

We continued to study chapter one in house group, where I received a second reminder from the Lord about the Healing Centre, after we had focused on the following text:

> *"Therefore, because of you, the heavens have withheld their dew and the earth its crops."*
> Haggai 1:10 (NIV)

As we entered into a time of prayer, I felt the Lord place something into my hands. It was a flower, containing small drops of dew and, as I looked at it, the flower increased in size until it became the size of a chalice in my hands. The drops of dew also increased until they were flowing over the edges of the flower chalice. I was holding it up and people came to drink from it. I knew that this dew, this water in the flower chalice in my hands, was Living Water. I felt a tremendous excitement about this chalice of Living Water that had been placed in my hands, for I knew it was so precious and it also had healing qualities. I also remembered that the flower image had been given to the Bethel Network group praying for the Healing Centre vision, some months earlier, so that it had become like a logo for the network.

> *"Jesus answered her, 'If you knew the gift of God and who it is that asks you for a drink, you would have asked him and he would have given you living water..... whoever drinks the water I give him will never thirst. Indeed the water I give him will become in him a spring of water welling up to eternal life."*
> John 4: 10, 13 (NIV).

But, why had the Lord placed this in my hands? Did he want me to carry the whole Bethel vision forward alone? Or maybe he was warning me that everyone else would go their own ways, leaving me as the lone vision carrier. In a sense, Bethel was different to Gilgal and Jericho, in that the main vision carriers for both those projects were other people

(Maria Blom for Gilgal and John Mallard for Jericho) and my role had been to support them. With Bethel, I have been given the vision, so I am the vision carrier and I am carrying it alone. Perhaps the Lord understood how isolating this can be and wanted to encourage me to hang on in there until the time was right. Whatever the reason, it was a powerful picture, which I could never forget – a vessel of living water. Was this Living Water to be made available to the people of Birmingham? Despite my excitement about it, I felt so inadequate to be the only person who was holding the chalice. It was such a responsibility.

Just this week, I was praying about this latest vision with another member of the Bethel Network. She reminded me of a prophecy that had been given at a "Revival Fires" evangelistic meeting in Dudley in 1999. It was a prophecy about the city of Birmingham (which is on tape, available from The Grace Centre, Dudley) and the woman who received the prophecy, Sue Mitchell, spoke the following words:

"But I see in the Spirit that the grace of Birmingham has been a chalice, a cup of the Lord. But it is a cup that has been filled with false drink. It is a poisoned chalice and the Lord shows me several streams into the city – false streams that have been dug by the hand of man and have been used by the heart of the enemy to fill this city with a poisoned drink. It has been cut off from a flow of life and a flow of pure water."

The prophecy went on to say that a new flow of life would be coming to the city that would be so great that Birmingham would be called "Brimming Town". The Lord was positioning nine diamonds at significant places around the city, each of which would manifest distinctive fruit, the nine fruits of the Spirit:

"And this is the fruit that will be squeezed into the cup. This is the fruit that will make the place sweet again. And it is the lives of God's people that are being squeezed out into the glory of their fruit that will again purify the city and sweeten the cup. So the Lord will raise up ministries..."

A city brimming over with the flow of God and his fruit!

This is a wonderful revelation that ministries would be raised up manifesting all the fruits of the Spirit:

Love, joy, peace, patience, kindness, goodness, meekness, gentleness and self control.

What a wonderful thing to look forward to!

And I have no doubt that Maria Blom's three-part prophecy of Gilgal, Jericho and Bethel are three of those diamonds mentioned in the Dudley prophecy. Ministries offering love and kindness to all kinds of people in the city: women and children, the disabled, victims of exploitation and/or violence, people caught up in criminal activity or prostitution or drug misuse, the long-term unemployed, the mentally ill, homeless people, others who have fallen on hard times, those who are in poverty, people with chronic illness – the list goes on…

Is the Lord now offering us a new way ahead, that is no longer a poisoned chalice but a cup, brimming over with Living Water!

In my last book ("I Will Lift up my Eyes"), I also described a poisoned chalice in the final chapter. The imagery for this was more on a global level, in which the present generation is leaving for future generations, a world that is polluted and being destroyed, with toxic air, a legacy of nuclear waste, a world with wrong values, selfishness, violence, exploitation and with corrupt political systems. How wonderful that God has given a prophecy that Birmingham will be turned around and, maybe after that, the rest of the world.

In that book ("I Will Lift up my Eyes"), a new form of society was described, "Civilisation 2000", which had certain qualities in line with Christian values and which was the antithesis of the negative issues expressed in the previous paragraph. The original thinking for such a society had been carried out by Barbara Panvel and I have joined her from time to time to work on some of these themes. In one initiative, which she named "HOPE", there has been a focus on health, arising from the ideas in two books: "The Ecology of Health" by Dr Robin Stott (Schumacher Briefing No. 3, Green Books, 2000) and "Health, Wealth and the New Economics: an agenda for a healthier world" by James Robertson (Ed.), a collection of papers and discussions from The Other Economic Summit (TOES) in 1985 and sponsored by the World Health Organisation.

Stott argues that our present NHS focuses on the treatment of disease, rather than on the wider issues which impact on an individual's health. These include: employment; social inclusion; healthy lifestyles; good housing; using renewable energy; phasing out pollutants; healthier transport styles; regional production of food; local participation in decision-making. He identifies a number of gulfs that need to be bridged: between narrow and broader definitions of health; between popular understanding of the causes of ill health and societal and scientific responses to these causes; between the wellbeing of the environment and the wellbeing of humans; between a society which pursues wealth in the hope of creating health; between 'power over', rather than 'power with' leadership; between locally-determined need and centrally-determined actions and between the rhetoric and reality of patient and citizen participation in the control and direction of their lives.

Robertson concludes that conventional economic policies are failing to create healthier societies and positively damage the health of many people in the world.

Barbara Panvel has been bringing together a number of other thinkers in this field, to work together on the themes of "Civilisation 2000". Her starting point is a definition of what constitutes a just and sustainable society. One small group, in which I participated, has focused on the issue of health and the Stott and Robertson theses. I believe that this work fits into the vision for the Bethel Healthy Living Centre and this is the reason I have included these paragraphs in this section, for work has already begun on this aspect of the vision.

I still hold the flower chalice in my hands and am seeking where the Lord wants me to present it to offer his Living Water of healing to those with no hope in their lives. Do pray for the fulfilment of his vision of a Healing Centre and a Healthy Living Centre.

CHAPTER FIVE

Drawing the three parts together.

God has been at work through Gilgal, Jericho and Bethel. Each story has shown how God envisioned his people, through revelation, then encouraged them to work together across Christian denominations to bring the vision about. And each story shows that God provided the resources of people and finance (sometimes from secular sources) that were needed. Each story also demonstrates that, when a revelation is of God, there are bound to be times of "reversal" in the progress of its fulfilment, during which it seems as if the project will never get off the ground and may even be lost. Perhaps these are caused by the work of Satan, but God uses them to show that he is behind the vision and that he will bring it about ultimately. These are times when God's people feel their own weakness and inadequacy, when God works to make them humble but he also uses the reversal to strengthen the faith of his people and to witness to his power before unbelievers.

And each of these stories has shown that God still performs miracles today. In Gilgal, it was the miracle of restoring a derelict building, providing the finances for it, turning around the mind of the sceptics and then using the building for his purposes, to help women and children and families in need in the city. For Jericho, it was the miracle of providing an alternative building (three times larger), when those opposing God's purposes had ensured that a chosen site was lost, then with the miracle of multiplying small "widow's mites" gifts of money into almost a million pounds, so that God's purposes for the long-term unemployed of the city could be fulfilled. For Bethel, the miracle will be in replacing a poisoned chalice with a new flower chalice, brimming over with living water, which will be used to heal the wounded of the city.

Each of these projects has touched the lives of many but even these are only a small proportion of the people of the city. But these stories represent a "new beginning" and the full working out of God's purposes for the city are still to be fulfilled. Remember, the 1999 Dudley prophecy spoke of nine diamonds. This book has described three and yet, even those three have divided to produce others, so that those involved have been bowled over by what God has done through them already. What might have been only three small projects has so far become fourteen (see diagram in Figure 1).

> *"Now to him who is able to do immeasurably more than all we ask or imagine, according to his power that is at work within us."*
> Ephesians 3:20.

I believe that these projects are about God's Kingdom being extended in the city. So often as Christians we get muddled up about the concept of God's Kingdom, thinking that his Kingdom is the Church. Many Christians expend much effort in trying to extend the Church when, all along God wants us out in the community amongst unbelievers, showing his love and compassion, being instruments of his healing power – extending his Kingdom there, especially amongst those who are poor, marginalized or damaged by their life experiences. And these projects have shown too, that in a city so much dominated by Islam, God has also used his people to express compassion and love towards those who are Muslims.

The beautiful thing about Gilgal and Jericho and their associated projects is that each of them is for the needy people of the city. Each project provides opportunities to show God's love in action – indeed, to manifest the first, and most important fruit of the Spirit, LOVE. This love has been expressed through Gilgal for women and children (and other needy parents and teenagers) and through Jericho for the long-term unemployed who have additional disadvantages in their lives.

| GILGAL | JERICHO | BETHEL |

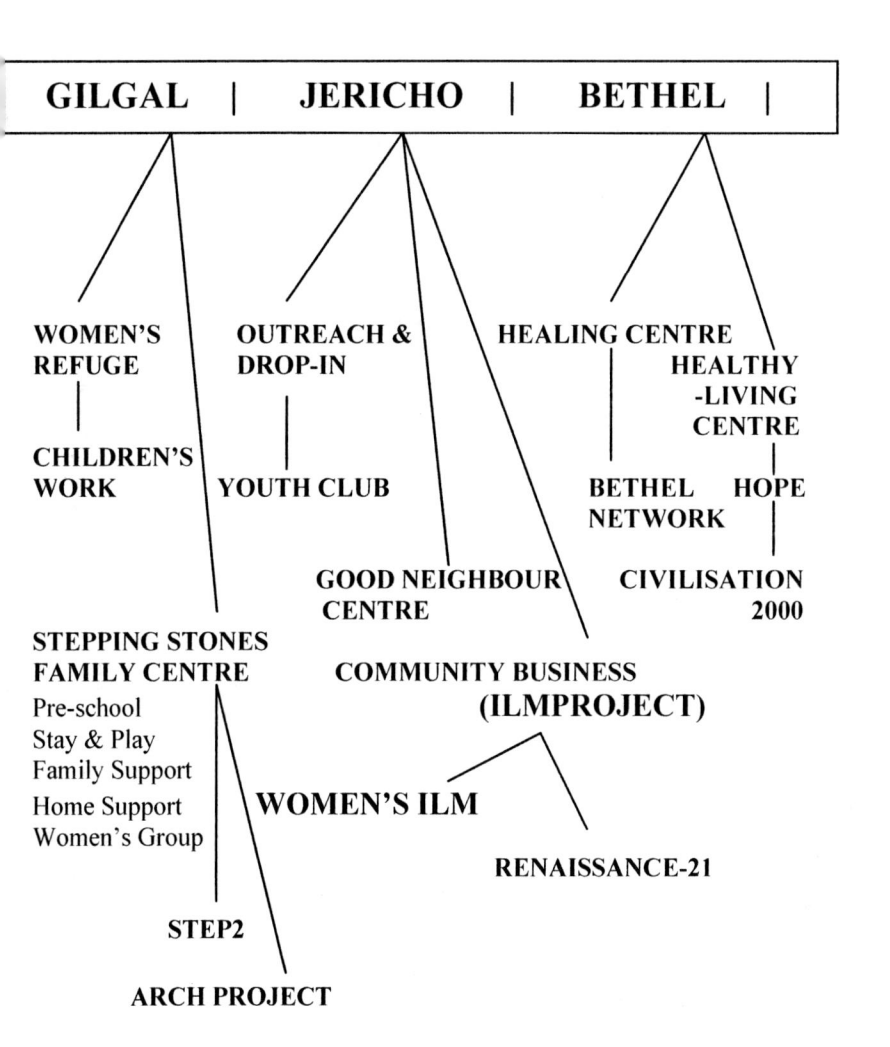

- **WOMEN'S REFUGE**
  - **CHILDREN'S WORK**
- **STEPPING STONES FAMILY CENTRE**
  - Pre-school
  - Stay & Play
  - Family Support
  - Home Support
  - Women's Group
  - **STEP2**
  - **ARCH PROJECT**

- **OUTREACH & DROP-IN**
  - **YOUTH CLUB**
- **GOOD NEIGHBOUR CENTRE**
- **COMMUNITY BUSINESS (ILMPROJECT)**
  - **WOMEN'S ILM**
  - **RENAISSANCE-21**

- **HEALING CENTRE**
  - **HEALTHY-LIVING CENTRE**
  - **BETHEL HOPE NETWORK**
  - **CIVILISATION 2000**

Figure 1: The proliferation of new projects from the original three-part prophecy

In telling the Gilgal story I described two pictures received by people in my own church that, I believe, have become prophetic. When first received, we thought they were just about Gilgal but they have proved true about Jericho too. The first picture was the one received by Eileen, when she saw vast crowds of people thronging the pavement – and Jesus was going among them, touching each person and healing them. The second picture was that received by John Wiltshire, in which the church congregation was inside a large building like an airport lounge with large windows. Outside were hoards of people in need of all nationalities; the people inside had everything they needed but the people outside were destitute.

I believe that the three names given to Maria Blom – Gilgal, Jericho and Bethel – were also significant when they are looked at in a Biblical context. The first two relate to places and events at the end of the forty years of wanderings of God's people in the wilderness, just as they were about to enter the Promised Land. Bethel comes from an earlier event, when God reminded Jacob that he was a part of the promise given to his grandfather, Abraham – that he would become the father of all nations and that all nations would be blessed through him. Each of the events in the Bible was accompanied by miraculous activities (the opening of the River Jordan, when it was in flood, the collapse of the walls of Jericho) or revelations (the ladder stretching up to heaven, with angels ascending and descending on it). And so it has been with these three projects – miraculous events (coincidences), unexpected windows of opportunity, the breaking down of opposition through prayer, rainbow visions, dreams, words of knowledge, divine appointments, revelations, visions of light, God giving a similar message to more than one person, the provision of financial resources, like manna from heaven (Eileen's golden bank notes floating down like leaves). There has been so much in common with the experiences of the Old Testament people. We are still a pilgrim people.

It is quite possible that some people reading these stories will think of them as fanciful and the pictures as figments of imagination. Some people do not believe that God communicates with his people these days through pictures, dreams and words of knowledge and so they might have trouble taking these stories on board (indeed, this was the attitude of one person at the first church meeting about the Gilgal vision). I hope this is not the case, as I believe that God uses such coincidences and miracles to build up the faith of his people and to witness to non-believers.

> *"When a prophet of the Lord is among you, I reveal myself to him in visions, I speak to him in dreams."*
> Numbers 12:6 (NIV)

> *"Let me tell about the visions and revelations I received from the Lord. I was caught up into the third heaven fourteen years ago. Whether my body was there or just my spirit, I don't know; only God knows. But I do know that I was caught up into paradise and heard things so astounding that they cannot be told.*
> 2 Cor. 12:1-4 (NLT)

> *"I am John...I was exiled to the island of Patmos for preaching the word of God and speaking about Jesus. It was the Lord's day, and I was worshipping in the Spirit. Suddenly, I heard a loud voice behind me, a voice that sounded like a trumpet blast. It said, 'Write down what you see, and send it to the seven churches...'"*
> Rev. 1:9-11 (NLT)

I thank God that the sceptical attitude did not prevail, for that would have meant that hundreds of needy people in the city would not have been helped. It is true that, sometimes, we think God is speaking to us when he isn't, and this can lead to much confusion and pain. It is therefore important to test every word of knowledge, prophecy or picture that is received, until there is no doubt about its source. This happened with Gilgal and Bethel, by independent revelations, and with Jericho and Bethel, through much collective prayer. In all three projects there have been fortuitous coincidences, which were more than chance occurrences, and the provision of funds when there were none.

Of necessity, I have had to write these stories from my own perspective and experiences of God revealing his purposes to me, during my own contemplative prayer life and prayer times with other Christians. I am so bound up in each of the stories that I could not tell them without some reference to myself and what I was doing and feeling at the time of each story; indeed, I am the only person who is involved in all three projects from the original prophecy. Yet, I do not want my readers to think that I played any other part than as God's instrument, albeit a fragile, frightened, despairing, tired, frustrated and blinkered one at times. There is no doubt in my mind that these projects happened despite me, not because of me – that God's hand is in each and that his purposes are being fulfilled through them. I feel privileged to have been so involved in the working out of God's plans through these three projects. When God first spoke to me in 1983 through Isaiah 35 ("the desert will rejoice and blossom as the rose"), I could never have believed that I would be a witness to so much taking place in the city of Birmingham at God's behest. It has been a wonderful experience, though difficult at times, and my own life has been transformed by it.

I have written and published these stories so that others can hear of God's modern-day miracles, so that their faith is also strengthened. I hope too, that the stories will encourage others who believe that God is speaking to them, and revealing his purposes to them, to listen to his voice, to seek independent confirmation that it is his voice and then to act in obedience to his leading and his calling.

When Jesus walked this earth, he performed many miracles and one of the reasons for this was that people would believe in him because of them.

"Jesus answered, 'I did tell you, but you do not believe. The miracles I do in my Father's name speak for me.'"
John 10:25 (NIV)

I do pray that the modern-day miracles I have described in this book will be believed and will speak of God still at work in our world today.

"Sing to the Lord a new song, for he has done marvellous things."
Psalm 98:1 (NIV)

Also by Christine Parkinson

This book will take you on a deep spiritual journey, whilst you travel with the author through the colourful cities of Kowloon, Manila, Singapore, Bangkok and Calcutta, meeting on the way some significant Christian pioneers of urban mission - Jackie Pullinger-To, Dorothy McMahon McCrae, Mother Teresa and others.

A challenging and provoking book that will not leave you unmoved.

ISBN 0755200470

Price £11.95

Available to order through all good bookshops or Internet bookstores or direct from the publisher at:
www.authorsonline.co.uk

40 Castle Street
Hertford
SG14 1HR
England

Printed in the United Kingdom
by Lightning Source UK Ltd.
99724UKS00001B/91-135